Count Otto's Dragon

DON BEMIS

OakTara

WATERFORD, VIRGINIA

Count Otto's Dragon

Published in the U.S. by:
OakTara Publishers
P.O. Box 8
Waterford, VA 20197

Visit OakTara at
www.oaktara.com

Cover design by Muses9 Design
Cover image man © 2008/Jupiterimages
Cover images © iStockphoto.com: cobalt background/The Stock Lab, knights/Mlenny Photography, dragon tail/MistikaS, small mouse/DeGrie Photo Illustration, big mouse/Jeka Gorbunov, scroll/kim258, shield/goldhafen, flag/xyno

Copyright © 2009 Don Bemis. All rights reserved.

ISBN: 978-1-60290-177-3

Count Otto's Dragon is a work of fiction. References to real people, events, establishments, organizations, or locales are intended only to provide a sense of authenticity and are used fictitiously. All other characters, incidents, and dialogue are drawn from the author's imagination.

To Lois,
again and always.

And to Ted DeRose,
for the book you gave me.

Acknowledgments

I never enjoyed history when I was young enough to get grades in it. History textbooks seem designed to suck the life out of the past, leaving it deader than its people. The subject only became interesting afterward when I started to see the "story" embedded within "history." I have now watched three generations of humanity behave like our predecessors as we become history for our descendants.

Obviously the book you hold is not true. However, it is a challenge to create "believable" fantasy. Some grounding in reality helps. The rise of the Church in Ireland is an especially interesting tale, where itinerant monks and missionaries preceded the organized Church with its priests and bishops. I would not have fully appreciated it but for a Christian friend, a teacher, who gave me a book to take along as I left home for a few months of consulting work. It was entitled, *The Spreading Flame: The Rise And Progress Of Christianity From Its First Beginnings To The Conversion Of The English,* by F.F. Bruce (1910-1990). The title is a mouthful, but the story is fascinating. After I read it, I passed the book on to somebody else. I hope they appreciate it as much as I did.

Enter the rollicking medieval world
of Count Otto and the dragon,
where everything seems to go hysterically wrong...
or is it right?

*For all those who not only like to chuckle,
but downright guffaw.*

One

High in an arched castle window, a gossamer lacework of spider's silk shimmered in the morning sun. A shining finger of sunlight laughed at the flimsy barrier, not even slowing down in its race through the room's dusty air to the opposite wall. The finger, bejeweled by lustrous bluebottle flies, seemed poised to write brilliant revelations in the greasy soot, but no words appeared. Instead it crept diagonally down the wall to a mousehole and peeped in. Finding nobody in residence, it departed that homely abode and picked its way through a herd of dust bunnies grazing on the floor.

The chamber was filled with music, hummed by flies in tremolo, and accompanied by a basso drone from the bed. The luminous finger pirouetted through a buzzing crowd of sparkling jewels lounging about a chamberpot and dipped in for a short swim. After emerging from the opposite side of the pool, the sunbeam played tag with a cockroach and jumped lightly onto the bed. It dried itself on a soiled sheet and commenced a pilgrimage across hills and dales of a wrinkled counterpane, apparently attracted by oracular snorts and whistles issuing from a recumbent Count Otto.

Finally it reached its goal. Glimmers of light erupted on the Count's stubbly cheek when the radiant finger reflected off a shimmering, vibrating puddle of drool by the corner of his open mouth. The sunbeam lovingly traced a line up his sagging jowl and tapped his puffy eyelid. "Wake up!" it beckoned soundlessly.

Count Otto winced when the solar finger gouged into his eye. Wincing made his eyebrows ache. "Not yet," snorted the back of his throat, but too loudly. The rest of him heard. He rolled over to flee the morning, but every part of his head seemed to move at a different speed. His slumber exploded in a series of painful throbs at about sixty collisions per minute. The faithful sunbeam followed him, settled on his earlobe, and played spotlight to a flea delving for dainties amongst the ear hairs.

Otto struck his ear with the flat of his hand. Then he bellowed. Although he was no physicist and had no intellectual interest in the effects of air compression inside an ear canal, he nonetheless observed that pain could result. The flea, more of a survivalist than a physicist, had already concluded that a moving hand was to be avoided. It dug deeper into the ear. Count Otto's head continued its rhythmic explosions at a slightly faster rate. His stomach churned in sympathy.

The Count stumbled out of bed. He was not in a good mood. His subjects, courtiers, and dogs knew to avoid him at such times. The chamberpot did not. It was new to the job, its predecessor having recently suffered an unfortunate accident involving stairs. It sat patiently in its master's path, awaiting his call. His foot found it. Flies erupted like fireworks. The enraged Count kicked with sufficient vigor to punish not only the faithful pot but a heavy chair behind it. The chair only wobbled, but the twirling vessel had a flair for the dramatic. It caromed through the bedchamber door, teetered over the edge of the landing, and expired on a flagstone floor eighteen feet below.

Count Otto limped to the window. Eight-legged seamstresses left off making burial shrouds for flies and scuttled into shadowy sanctuaries between the stones. He leaned heavily on the sill to take the weight off his throbbing foot. The flea chose that moment to resume mining. Balancing between his right hand and left foot, the Count reached for his ear with his left hand. A displaced bedbug began to embed itself in his right armpit. The Count tried to balance on his good foot so he could deal with both attackers simultaneously, but it did not work.

His brain was not up to managing such a balancing act. Down went the bad foot. It would just have to get used to the pain, he decided. Peering blearily outward while scratching at his ear with one hand and extracting the bedbug with the other, Otto observed a couple of serfs watching with amusement. Their taxes would go up if he could get their names.

However, they would have nothing worth taxing if the view through the window was any indication. A filthy town lay to his right. Blighted farmland was to his left. All that he beheld was his by right of birth, from the dead bugs on the windowsill to the swamp on the horizon. Well, nearly all. Otto could not command the sun to stay out of his eyes.

His bedchamber was on the eastern side of the castle. Ten feet below the window he shared with the spiders, a twelve-foot-thick stone wall extended southward to the town gate. It continued on for a distance before bending clockwise on its mission to encapsulate the town and reconnect to the castle's northeast corner. The windowless east face of the castle, including the west wall of the bedroom, completed the fortification. Soldiers in a garrison beneath his feet could swarm onto the wall like bees, if they were paying attention. Usually they were not.

Otto thought again, as he had often thought before, that his window was not well situated for defense. The earlier Count who built the castle had been more concerned about the view. Perhaps the old Count was right. He had been assassinated by an ambitious nephew, not shot through the window by enemy archers. The nephew, in his turn, had succumbed to plague rather than attackers.

The wall below the window was only ten feet high on the

town side, but the outer face loomed twenty-four feet from the caps of the battlements to the surface of the moat. The eastern hillside had been cut away a few centuries earlier when slaves cost less, in order for the moat to fully encircle the town. Water would not flow uphill, even for a Count. Only a narrow spine of the original hillside had been left for a causeway to the drawbridge. The stone-lined moat was twenty feet wide and had once been twelve feet deep. Garbage floated on the surface. Anything that seagulls were too proud to eat would eventually sink. About four feet of refuse had met that humiliating end since the moat was last cleaned sixty years earlier after sheep were seen grazing on it.

In a sense, this had been Otto's room for his entire life. He had been conceived here before taking up residence in the nursery, migrating after a few years to a room down the hall, and eventually moving back into the quarters where he had started. If things went well, he might die peacefully in the same bed. His father had done the same, as had his father before him, et cetera. The view through the window had hardly changed for any of them. The only difference was that now both the nursery and the room down the hall were unoccupied.

"Four o'clock and all's well!" The watchman's cry floated from the top of the gatehouse.

The town had indeed awakened long before Otto had, but he knew it was not that late—or that early. The sun would not be shining in his window at four o'clock. The watchman tended to announce the hour whenever he remembered to and occasionally would toss in a couple of extra hours just in case. He would start over after reaching twelve. Whatever the time really was, beggars were already at their posts, as were dogs to growl at them. It had been at least an hour since chamberpots more fortunate than that of the Count had been emptied through windows into the street.

A group of serfs dragged the bloated carcass of a mule up

the muddy track. The mule was heavy, and they were few. They did not look forward to hauling it all the way to a smoldering dump outside of town. Men and mule disappeared into the shadowed arch of the gateway that penetrated the wall. They reappeared beyond it a minute later, tugging their cargo onto the drawbridge. Halfway across, they halted and looked around. The watchman was watching maids, not the road. The bearers furtively tipped their load into the moat. A plume of black water shot up like a blossom, opened like a flower, and scattered petals of muck and mire onto fleeing serfs. The watery bloom withered as swiftly as it had grown, but not fruitlessly. The mule emerged like a hairy turnip and bobbed placidly beneath the bridge.

That'll keep the monster happy, thought the Count. Then he remembered: he had no monster. It had crawled out of the moat last Midsummer's Eve to escape from leeches but had become disoriented and wandered into the swamp. Mosquitoes had sucked it dry. *Oh, well*, Otto decided, *maybe raiders won't care to swim with a dead mule either.*

He turned away from the window. Where was his chamberlain? Clean clothing had not been laid out in place of his dirty ones.

"Things just don't get any better than this," the Count muttered. He was reduced to peeling off his own grimy nightshirt. He donned greasy clothes from the day before with his own hands, which were unaccustomed to such activity. A few buttons got missed. His feet managed to find their way into the proper slippers after only two tries, but the bruised toes on his right foot were in no mood to congratulate him. Otto's toilette was as complete as it could be under the circumstances. Uttering imprecations against the chamberlain, he hobbled downstairs.

Nobody was in the great hall but a surly maid scrubbing the floor where the chamberpot had landed. No, there was one other person. Seated by the fire with a mug by his left hand and a book in his right, was a small man made gray by years of dust from field and road, clad in a plain gray robe, and topped with a halo of tonsured gray hair. The halo was thinning a bit in the front and soon would resemble a horseshoe.

The man arose and turned gray eyes toward the approaching Count.

"Ah, Friar Fred!" Otto's voice bounced around the inside of his skull. He would have to speak more quietly for a while. "Welcome. But why is Father Frank not here instead? Today is the day for the blessing of the ale. I wanted him to pray for a headache besides."

The friar inspected the bleary Count. "Then there is no need. I can see that the ale was fine, and you have already been granted a headache. But as to ..." Friar Fred blinked and looked away. He coughed. "Alas, Father Frank is no longer with us. He was eaten yestereve by a dragon."

The Count stared at his guest. "Not in the town, I hope!"

"Nay. In Yonder Wood over yonder. The Father had read a book about Saint Francis preaching to the animals. Saint Francis was his namesake. Father Frank was a bit discouraged because people seemed not to listen, so he decided to see if beasts would do better. I went also. 'Why not just preach to cows or chickens or something else in town?' I asked him. 'The woods may be thick with dragons.' "

"'Dragons, shmagons!' said Father Frank." The friar halted and drained his mug. The grumbling maidservant arose from her scrubbing long enough to refill it for him. He blessed her, and she returned to scrubbing and grumbling.

"Shmagons?" asked the Count. "That doesn't sound like priestly talk."

"I think he got it from the rabbi."

The Count was puzzled. "He talks—er, talked—to the rabbi?"

6

"Indeed. They would get together, talk religion, and make up jokes. Sometimes an old Druid would join them."

"What sort of jokes?"

"Surely you've heard them. They usually started off like, 'A priest, a rabbi, and a Druid were fishing together,' or some such thing."

"Oh, *those* jokes. I wondered where they came from. But back to the dragon."

"Ah, yes," said the friar. "No sooner had the Father spoken than there was a horrible flutter of wings, and a monstrous dragon landed on the path. It licked its lips with a forked tongue, from both sides at the same time, toward the middle. 'I am Shmagon,' it said. 'How good of you to call me to dinner!' "

"Father Frank flinched not. 'Nay!' he said. 'I have come to preach to you.' But the dragon cared not for theology. He was a gentleman, though. He allowed the priest to make his confession to me before supper." The friar paused. "I took as long as I could, but as soon as the Father had finished repenting of his jokes, he was out of fresh sins."

"Then the dragon asked me to say grace, and we all bowed our heads. Mind you, I was fair flustered. Every mealtime prayer fled from me, but for one from my youth before I took Holy Orders. I tried to recall a better one, but the dragon's tail began to twitch."

"'Hurry!' the Father whispered. 'I am ready. But the dragon may also crave fresh friar if he gets too hungry.' So I recited, 'Good bread, good meat, good Lord, let's eat.' 'Amen,' said the dragon, and he barbecued the Father and gobbled him on the spot. It was that fast. I doubt Father Frank felt a thing." The friar bowed his head. There was silence. Even the surly maid ceased grumbling.

"He was a good priest," the Count finally said.

"The dragon said likewise."

Otto shook his head. That was a mistake. Fresh pounding

7

erupted in his temples. "I always told Father Frank that reading was dangerous. But it is too late now for him to learn. We should find his mortal remains and give him a decent burial."

"I think not," demurred Friar Fred. "Good dragons waste no food, and you have one of the best. Whatever you should find of the Father would be unfit for the churchyard, if you get my drift."

"Oh, I see." The Count was slightly relieved for two reasons. First, a perilous quest would not be necessary. Second, the fields might have blight and the moat might lack a monster, but at least his county had one of the best dragons. That would give him some bragging rights the next time all the counts got together.

He was suddenly jolted back to reality. "Next time" would be the County Convention, at his castle, in one week. Nothing was ready. The Chief Steward who usually arranged such affairs had unfortunately referred to the portly Duke Puckett of Aard as "Bucket of Lard" a fortnight earlier after the Duke had presumably departed from a visit to the castle (but hadn't), and the Count had been obliged to consign the steward to the dungeon. Releasing the prisoner had been on his list of things to do, but annual ale-testing responsibilities were higher up the list. Hence the headache.

Now he had two headaches, which might explain why his head felt like it was splitting in two. The Chief Steward had authority over the servants and thus could make even a nobleman's life miserable. Two weeks in the dungeon might have left him a little grumpy. It would take a higher authority than the Count to keep the steward in line. The Duke obviously would not do.

Otto turned to the little gray friar who represented the highest authority of all. "Er, Friar Fred," he began, "I have a question for you."

"Yes?"

"Father Frank spoke often of forgiveness. Do you believe likewise?"

"Indeed I do."

"If a person did not wrong another person, but the other believes he has been wronged, should he forgive the first person anyway? Even if he doesn't need forgiven?"

The Friar cocked his head. "I should say yes, I think. That is, if I understand aright."

"Good! Would you come with me? There is a man who needs to hear this."

The Count led the friar from the great hall to a gloomy service passage at the back. A small high window at the far end traded a bit of daylight for smoke from sconces that flickered along the side wall. Otto lifted a lamp from its hook and limped onward. The kitchen was to the left, discernible by the smell of meat going bad. Storerooms full of onions, garlic, and vinegar competed for attention from the right side.

Almost at the end of the passage, the Count detoured into an arched doorway on the left. It led not into a room but onto the upper landing of a stairway that disappeared leftward into shadows. The men descended a steep, dark flight of uneven steps. If one stumbled, he would dash himself against the stone wall at the foot of the stairway. Nobody stumbled.

They turned left again at the bottom and stepped into an unlighted passage. The Count and the friar proceeded rightward, accompanied by a small pool of flickering yellow light. They were retracing their steps from half a minute before, but twelve feet lower. Doors on the left side of the dismal hall led into storerooms piled with three centuries' worth of things that somebody had thought might come in handy someday. Otto had enjoyed exploring those rooms when he was a boy, but he hardly thought of them anymore.

Just then a cacophony of squeaks and undulating squeals issued through a closed door to the right of the men.

"What is that?" asked Friar Fred.

"The wine cellar."

"Does it always whine so?"

"In good years, yes."

The Count pushed the door open and held the light aloft. It flared a little, almost tasting alcohol in the musky air thick with smells of wood, old grapes, and fermentation. Nearly all the way around the room, racks from floor to ceiling supported rows of dusty oaken barrels. A bench stood by the door. Assorted taps and a mallet rested upon it. In the middle of the room stood a purple-stained table, surrounded by four chairs and surmounted by four upside-down goblets. Against one goblet leaned three purple rats, wobbling on their hind legs and squealing in lusty harmony. One made a tiny hiccup. The other two chittered in seeming laughter, then resumed their serenade.

The friar saw the source of their merriment. A recently tapped barrel drip-drip-dripped onto the floor. Swarms of rats were drinking from the puddle, wallowing in it, or stumbling in all directions. Every rat seemed to have something important to say unless it was actively engaged in drinking or sleeping. A few violently disagreed with each other; others fervently agreed with each other. Rats slouched on barrel racks. Rats slept in corners. One rat skidded off the top of a barrel, bounced off Friar Fred's tonsured pate, and staggered to the puddle without so much as an apology.

"'Tis a very good year, methinks," said the Friar. He looked upward toward the place where his rat had launched and noticed beyond it a ladder that extended to a wooden hatch in the ceiling. "Where does that go?"

"The kitchen. Barrels are raised and lowered through there. But enough of this place. We have other business." Otto departed the cellar with the friar in his wake.

The noise diminished when the door was shut; it disappeared entirely when the men turned right at a corner in the passage. A barred door blocked their way twenty feet ahead. A large block of wood stood by the wall. A battleaxe and a pike leaned against the block. Four feet in front of the door, a smoky lamp shared a wooden table with two mugs and a checker board. Two pale, burly men intently studied the board.

When the Count cleared his throat, both men jumped up. One grabbed the axe. Sparks flew from its blade as it dragged across the floor. The other took hold of the pikestaff, which jammed between the floor and the low ceiling. He tugged ineffectually at it.

"Some Dungeon Master you are!" muttered the man with the axe.

"Some headsman you are!" growled the other. "Dulling thy tool so."

The Count slowly shook his head at the scene but not slowly enough. A fresh series of throbs erupted. "To the Chief Steward," he commanded, but not softly enough.

The Dungeon Master hoisted an iron bar from the door and set it against the wall with a clang. It was not a quiet clang. The headsman pulled the squealing door open.

Otto winced. "Oil those hinges!"

"Now, my lord?"

"Yes!"

"Certainly, my lord." The headsman lifted the lamp from the table. He dribbled some oil from the spout onto both hinges and returned the lamp to its place. He swung the door open and shut a few times. It protested loudly at first (as did Otto's head) but settled down shortly (which Otto's head did not). Finally,

11

pulling the door fully open one more time, the Dungeon Master and his lamp preceded them through the black opening.

Once they were inside, light flickered off the wall at more or less the same rate as the Count's headache. The headsman banged the door shut behind them. The bar thudded into place. The Count's brain thudded in sympathy.

Stone walls rose immediately to their left and front, and blackness to the right. The Dungeon Master led them that direction down a steep stairway. His lamp reflected feebly from the damp floor and walls. At the bottom, a passage stretched forward, defined by a series of arches three feet wide and barely higher than their heads. The arches pierced parallel walls four feet thick and four feet apart. Stone slabs formed an uneven ceiling generally less than seven feet above the floor. It was higher in some places, lower in others, depending upon the thickness of the slabs. They had only been smoothed on one side to make the floor above. Appearance was not important in a dungeon. It was a necessity like a well or a cesspool—an interruption in the rock that supported the castle's weight.

On either side of the passage, heavy wooden doors bound with rusting iron were set into gaps between the walls. Each door had a little barred hatch at eye height that could be opened to slide food and water in, or to watch a prisoner starve, depending on how a person outside the cell felt. Shadows from the arches obscured all but the nearest cell doors. A faint cough echoed from a distant cell. The friar vaguely saw that as black as the place was, an even blacker pit was at the far end of the passage. It would not do to run the wrong direction here.

The Dungeon Master unlocked the first door on the left. The Count winced when the protesting door squealed open. Bluish light shot from the room. It would not have seemed bright in the world above, but in the dungeon it was dazzling.

Curious, Friar Fred ducked through the doorway. The cell was ten feet from front to back. Where the back wall met the ceiling, a shaft about six inches square sloped upward fifteen or twenty feet to the ground outside. The bluish brilliance was only a late morning sky shining into an area otherwise devoid of illumination. A pallid man was seated on a small chair behind a tiny table below the light. As soon as he noticed the friar, he became even paler and gripped the edge of the table.

"I did not expect light," the friar said over his shoulder.

"There is also fresh water when it rains," explained the Count. "This is the luxury cell for my finest prisoners, including Chief Stewards."

The rigid prisoner, well dressed for a man in his surroundings, continued to stare at the friar.

"The Steward is not the only man to speak of the Duke as he did," the Count said, "but he is the only one the Duke heard. May Lord Puckett soon find somebody else to be angrier at, in some other county."

"The Duke cares more for the animals in his menagerie than for men," muttered the Chief Steward. He transferred his attention to the Count. "You do not mean to kill me?"

"Nay. Good stewards do not grow on trees, and I shall not hang one from a tree either." A little flattery could not hurt.

"Then why do you bring a cleric if not to shrive me before I die?"

Count Otto shrugged. "Be shriven if you will, but not to die. I have need of you. The County Convention is in a week, and no preparations have been made in your absence. You are free."

The Chief Steward relaxed a bit. He thought for a moment. "I shall stay here."

The Count was stunned. So much for flattery! He turned to the jailer and was about to have the prisoner dragged to freedom, but the puzzled friar interrupted. "Why would you choose to remain in this foul place?"

"So I may keep a head with which to know the place is foul. If the Duke should come to the Convention and see me about, I would be a shorter man. As might you, my Lord."

Otto blanched. The steward had made his point.

"But it is not as bad as it may seem. Peddlers cannot trouble me here with their potions and brooms. I have light. I eat and drink well enough. My cell is cleaned daily and is two feet larger than the others. I even have furniture. After all, I am the Chief Steward, and the servants know to whom they will answer if I should ever go free!"

"Well, then, if you can direct the servants from here for yourself, you can direct them from here for your lord! The jailers shall be your messengers. Come, Friar!" Count Otto spun on his heel and left the cell. "Lock him up!"

The Dungeon Master hesitated. "But, my lord, the friar..."

Friar Fred had remained inside the cell. That was the trouble with holy men. They didn't follow orders well. Otto sighed and shook his head. It throbbed anew.

Meanwhile, the friar contemplated the prisoner. "Will you be shriven?"

"Nay. In my lord's black mood, he may decide to have my head if my soul is cleaned. Go."

Friar Fred blinked and exited. The Dungeon Master locked the cell, and the passageway again seemed black despite the torch. It took awhile for their eyes to readjust to the darkness.

The men felt their way up the steep steps and hallooed for the headsman to open the door. After half a minute that felt like half an hour, they heard the bar being lifted, and a creak as the door pivoted outward. The stale air around the jailers' post seemed almost fresh after the closeness of the dungeon.

The Dungeon Master dropped the bar back into place and drew his seat back to the checker table. He stared at the board. "Hoy! Thou moved a king whilst I was below!"

"Did not!"

"Did so!"

The Count and the friar left the debaters to debate and turned leftward at the corner of the passage.

Suddenly Friar Fred stopped. "How quiet it is!"

"We turned a corner."

"Nay, 'tis not that! Why are not the vermin singing?"

Otto listened. Surely enough, there was no sound but angry jailers. He pushed open the wine cellar door and held the lamp aloft. The rats remained where they had been, but not a one was moving. There was not even a squeaky snore. Friar Fred picked up one of the three erstwhile singers by its tail and sniffed its face. He dropped it and wiped his fingers on the belt of his cassock. "Poisoned!"

Count Otto would have gone pale if there had been enough light to go pale in. He started to swear but remembered the friar and crossed himself instead. As soon as that was taken care of, he inspected the dripping barrel. "Aye, something was poured through the vent hole in the top."

He went to the bench by the door. Taking a mallet and spare tap in one hand and a lamp in the other, he pushed through dirt and spiders to a far corner of the room. Cobwebs flashed and frizzled in the flame as he passed. He stopped at a

15

dusty barrel. "This one has not been touched."

Otto set the tap against the bung plug and pounded with the mallet. His head felt like it was being pounded also, but that could not be helped. The plug popped into the barrel, and the tap popped into the hole. The Count returned to the poisoned barrel and hammered the top of the tapered valve. The dripping stopped. Then he smashed off the valve handle and returned the mallet to the bench.

"No one must know of our discovery lest we alarm the villain, whoever he is. People will think this tap was broken by accident, and they will draw from the other instead." Otto hoisted a purple rat by the tail and dropped it into the tainted barrel. Friar Fred joined suit.

Even after Count and cleric had spent fifteen minutes pickling rodents, tails and attached carcasses continued to droop beyond their reach. Otto debated whether they should retrieve those also, but his burbling stomach and throbbing head vetoed the idea. "Oh, well, there are always *some* dead rats about." He turned to leave.

"The villain perhaps has kept the cheese safe for a while," observed the dusty friar to the cobwebby Count as they shut the door behind.

Two

Three days later, Count Otto paced back and forth, back and forth, on the second floor of the castle. This low-ceilinged mezzanine level was not intended for public use. Narrow hallways connected balconies and alcoves that overlooked larger rooms on the main floor. The balconies were in case the Count wanted to be seen, and alcoves with screens and lattices were in case he didn't. He didn't at the moment.

Preparations for the convention were not going well. Problems multiplied more rapidly than solutions. A barrel of honey had been spilled down the main staircase, attracting even more ants and flies than usual. Hunting hounds had somehow been put into the henhouse instead of the kennel. An unsightly hornets' nest outside a window had been removed with a rock. It bounced in through the window, and the hornets were not amused.

The lowering rope for the main chandelier had somehow been partially cut through, and the undamaged remainder was not up to the task. Two hundred pounds of wood, iron, and wax dropped onto the spot where the master of the feast would be seated in four days. A new chandelier had to be built. The shattered furniture beneath it was recycled as firewood. As emergency replacements, a huge moldy table and chairs to match were dragged upstairs from a storeroom where they had languished three generations for the crime of being ugly.

"One o'clock and all's well!" called a voice outside.

The Count disagreed. A hundred servants were busily accomplishing nothing, but he reflected that the place seemed empty nonetheless. It had felt that way ever since Countess Anna had died two years earlier. Two years to the day, in fact. Otto stopped. Below him in the reception hall, the surly maid was grumbling and scrubbing the floor. Her appearance was more attractive than her disposition. He took a seat in an alcove and watched through the screen. He wondered. It *had* been two years. He *was* a Count. Maybe he should....

His contemplation was broken by heavy pounding on the front door. The first and second door wardens ran into the reception hall from a side chamber, but they were too late. The door splintered into pieces and crashed open. In the doorway stood seven Vikings. Three of them held a battering ram. Two bore a ladder. One carried a tallow candle nearly half his own height and girth.

"Greetings!" boomed the seventh, a big man with plaited blond hair and a forked, plaited beard. His head sported an iron helmet with a sharpened ox horn protruding from either side. Strapped to his belt were a broadsword, an axe, and a quiver of arrows. Across his back was a bow. He wore leather boots with iron toes, and his leather jerkin was fortified with metal plates. A bronze and gold gorget protected his throat. In one hand he carried a whip; in the other, the end of a rope. His men were similarly attired, except for the whip and the rope.

"I am Ülf, a trader from Oslo, here to offer this lovely candle" (he nodded toward it) "free to you" (he nodded toward the first door warden) "in return for demonstrating our new cleaning tools." He tugged on the rope. A dozen tattered serfs, tied at the waist, stumbled into view. They carried rags, pails, and brooms. "We will clean out one room in your castle free of charge."

"Tell him we're busy," the first door warden directed the second door.

"Um, we're awfully busy right now," began the second door warden.

A Viking flung him into the first door warden, and the visitors stormed in. The serfs set to work scrubbing the floor as soon as the chief cracked his whip. The Viking with the candle parked his gift in a corner, and all seven commenced a quick but thorough appraisal of the room's furnishings. Into a sack went a set of silver candlesticks. So did a collection of jeweled mugs. The ladder went up, and a huge tapestry came down. A cracked portrait of grandsire Connoc the Cross-eyed stayed where it was.

"We will return these items as soon as they are properly cleaned," boomed Ülf, with a wink to his men. "I can see all of your rooms will need similar cleaning." He took a grubby rag from one serf and held it up for all to see. "Look at that! Filth, even after yon maid has cleaned!" He pointed toward the surly maid, who had not stopped scrubbing and grumbling.

Her head jerked up. "How *dare* you!" She flew to her feet and stormed toward him. "Filth, indeed!"

"Oho, a feisty one!" The Vikings guffawed.

She paid no attention to them but yanked the chief's helmet off by one of its horns, flipped it upside down, and embedded the other horn in the top of his head. He crashed to the floor.

The other Vikings went silent. The serfs stopped scrubbing to watch. The surly maid pulled the fallen chief's sword from its scabbard and inspected the blade. She turned flashing eyes on the live Vikings. "You want filth? Look at this blade! I'll wager it hasn't been cleaned since you left Norway! It's disgusting!" She flung it whirling into the corner. It sliced the top off the candle and clanged into the wall.

"Well, let's see *your* blades," she demanded. "Are they as bad?"

The men sheepishly drew out their swords. They were.

"As I thought! If your cleaning service is so good, surely they can clean your weapons for you!"

19

"Why didn't *we* think of that?" asked a Viking. He undid his sword and handed it to a serf. He examined the rest of his weapons and unfastened them also. The other Vikings followed suit.

The surly maid retrieved the sword she had thrown away and marched within six inches of the nearest Viking. He was half a head taller than she was, but he cowered anyway. She immediately backed away and looked on him with loathing. "Phew! Your jerkin stinks! You'll never attract maidens smelling like that! Off with it!"

He complied, as did the others.

"And I don't doubt your boots and leggings are as bad. Hand them over."

The warriors stripped to their woolen undergarments and looked questioningly at her.

"No, I wouldn't touch the rest of those things! Just pile everything else over there. Hats too."

The serfs looked at the swords. They picked them up. Then they looked at their ropes. They cut them.

"So *that's* why," said the Viking who had spoken earlier.

A serf plopped a helmet onto his head. "Look at me! I'm a Viking!" He spun in a circle, swinging his sword.

Woolen Vikings cowered like sheep.

"Take that thing off your head!" ordered the surly maid. "You'll get lice!"

"I already have lice," the serf said but obeyed anyway.

The maid glared at the huddled Vikings. "Well, you said you'd clean a room. Start cleaning. Take that dead thing outside, and get this blood off the floor before it stains!"

Two Vikings, supervised by a serf, dragged out the body of their chief.

The surly maid rounded on another Viking. "If you think the candlesticks are so dirty, you can polish them! And *you* (she pointed at another) can do the rest of the silver. And *you* and *you,*" she indicated the last two, "can beat the dust out of the tapestry!"

They dragged it out the doorway, laid it over a hedge, and beat it with sticks. Dust flew. A pair of armed serfs supervised the coughing, sneezing Vikings from the upwind side.

Otto left the scene long enough to bar the door to a balcony that also overlooked the reception hall, just in case some Viking should choose an emergency exit. Then he returned to the alcove and watched unobserved. A Viking scrubbed iron grillwork not two feet in front of the Count but did not see him through the coarse curtain. Alcoves were poorly lighted for a reason.

All of the cleaning was done within an hour.

"Now put it all back as it was," ordered the surly maid. "Except the portrait. It's ugly. Take it away!" Then she ordered them out of the castle.

"Begging your pardon, ma'am," begged a Viking, "but can we have our things back?"

"After they are cleaned, I'll think about it," she retorted. "But you can take that candle. It clashes with the décor."

Otto moved upstairs to watch through the bedroom window. The Vikings slunk down the street in their filthy woolies, dragging their fallen chief, decapitated candle, and Connoc the Cross-eyed with them. They were escorted to the bridge by a dozen serfs with broadswords and axes. Completing the parade was a crowd of jeering townspeople.

A Viking longboat floated in the moat. A plank extended from deck to shore. The mainsail was furled, and shields hung from the sides of the craft. A pile of candles was lashed to the afterdeck. The boat's fearsome bow, carved and painted to resemble a sea monster, bobbed head-high at the bridge. A rope secured the neck of the monster to the bridge's lifting chain. The impression was something like a very dangerous dog tied to a fence.

"How did *that* get there?" asked the town watchman, wondering if this might reflect poorly on his career.

"It has wheels. We had to pull it from the seacoast," replied a serf with a sword.

The incredulous watchman stared at him. "But that's eight leagues!"

"And two furlongs."

The Vikings slid down the embankment with their cargo. They boarded their vessel via the plank and drew it on deck behind them. Gently they laid their captain on the plank and bore him to a pile of sails at the foot of the mast. After arranging him with the candle lying on one side and Connoc on the other, all but the former candle bearer clambered up the wooden monster's neck onto the drawbridge.

The remaining Viking looked at the crowd of townspeople. "Does anybody have a light?" he pleaded. The gatekeeper dug a firebrand from a pile of burning trash and tossed it onto the deck. Sparks flew.

"Thank you." The Viking picked up the flaming stick. He poked at the end of the candle until some wick was exposed, and lit it. Tallow dripped onto the pile of sails. He touched his firebrand to the pile, which ignited immediately. Then he lit the rest of the candles, plus the mainsail for good measure, and scrambled onto the drawbridge just as flames shot up the rigging. Burning ropes snapped in two and flailed like fiery serpents. The crackling boom thudded to the deck.

The Viking borrowed a serf's sword long enough to cut the boat free. He sadly patted the monster's wooden head and shoved it away from the bridge. The six surviving Vikings sang a dirge heavily laden with umlauts while their captain's funeral pyre floated toward the corner of the moat.

"Now how will we get home?" asked a woolly Viking after the dirge was done.

"Oops!"

Their problems were not yet over. The surly maid ran out the gate with a broom. "Aren't you gone yet? Scat! Shoo!" She flailed at them, and they pelted down the road.

Count Otto reconsidered his earlier thoughts about the surly maid. Abstinence was safer.

The Vikings had no sooner come abreast of Pigtruffle Thicket, a twenty-acre stand of oak trees three furlongs distant, than a pack of nearsighted wolves bounded out and mistook them for sheep.

The wolves coughed up long johns for three days and left the county immediately afterward.

Three

Far up the river from Otto's county, Count Rollo the Clueless governed a nearly inaccessible valley on the west side of the Craggy Mountains. Remoteness had led to a bizarre culture and a nearly incomprehensible dialect. Rollo's subjects rarely ventured even as far as the Duckyard, their name for the vast Duchy of Aard on the eastern side of the range. Most of them preferred to stay home and mangle the language.

Their Count was awakened one morning by a crash. It wasn't the first, and maybe he should have been used to them, but he was annoyed anyway. It seemed a bit much to have to put up with things flying into his bedchamber three mornings in a row.

The first day it had been a sheep. Rollo had never seen a flying sheep. The sheep wasn't very good at it, either. It was dead.

The next morning, Rollo had no sooner left his bed than a tree sailed through the window and replaced him. A pine tree, to be precise, once about twelve feet tall, but twelve feet long as it reclined.

This day a boulder had dropped in. It missed the window and came through the wall instead.

The grumbling Count tugged at the bell sash. Nothing happened. Nothing had happened when he pulled it the day before either, or even the day before that. It must have broken when the sheep ran into it, he decided. He would have to find another bedroom until the sash could be repaired.

"Hey, Chamberlain!" Count Rollo called.

A thump in the hall was followed by a knock at the door.

"C'mon in! It ain't locked!"

The door opened. A cadaverous fellow entered, cracking the knuckles on his large hands.

The Count stared at him. "Who're *you?*"

"Your chamberlain, my lord."

"No, you ain't! My chamberlain ain't half your size."

"I am sorry, my lord, but your last chamberlain is dead." The new chamberlain cracked his knuckles again.

"He *is?* How in tarnation did he do that?"

"He choked to death, my lord."

"Well, I'll be thunderstruck!" exclaimed Rollo, thunderstruck. "Oh, well, cain't be helped. Dress me."

"With a will, my lord." The chamberlain walked briskly behind the Count and grasped the shoulders of his robe. With quivering hands, he started to lift it over the Count's head but then twisted his palms toward Rollo's neck. At that moment an anchor flew through the hole the boulder had made, and the chamberlain was terminally dashed against a large wooden wardrobe.

Rollo stared at the wreckage. "Grandma's dresser! That done it!" He grabbed the nearest tunic, yanked it on, and stomped out, slamming the door shut behind him. The bedchamber collapsed into rubble.

The furious Count strapped on a dagger and stormed out the front door of the castle.

A splashing noise beyond the town wall caught the Count's attention, so he exited through the gate to investigate. The drawbridge was dented, and a small tidal wave seemed to have flattened the grass alongside the moat, but nothing else looked out of the ordinary.

"Howdy do, Boss!" A serf stood not far past the bridge, sucking on a sprig of hay. He leaned against a poplar tree embedded upside down in a field. Shattered branches lay about.

25

"Howdy yerself!" Rollo called back. "Sump'n wrong with y'all's tree?"

"'Tain't my tree. Wuzzn't here yestiddy, in fact." The serf fingered one of the leaves. "Seems a mite peaked, don't it?"

"Reckon it come from springin' up so fast. Seed musta been kittywampus, too."

The serf shrugged. "Prob'ly figgered it better grow up quick or git squashed."

"Whatcha mean?"

"On account o' this field, I mean." The serf transferred the straw to the other side of his mouth. "Rocks keep poppin' up overnight. If that tree'da took its time, it mighta got run into."

Rollo contemplated. "Hmm, might be right. All them rocks make a beeline toward where the river runs outa the woods over yonder. An' the poor tree's right in line with 'em. Wonder if there's some sorta root under here pops up rocks like rutabagas." He turned around and eyed the scene he had left. "Right in line with my bedroom 'crost the moat there, too. Reckon I oughta see what's at t'other end an' git it dug up before it hurts sump'n." He ambled toward the woods.

The serf stayed behind. He spat out his straw and replaced it with a wilted leaf.

It was a glorious day for a walk. The sun shone brightly. Birds sang. Bees buzzed. A cow mooed overhead. A swarm of butterflies took wing when something thudded to earth in their midst. The trail to the woods was not too bad except where it crossed the line of rocks. Occasionally something more interesting than a rock would show up, like a shattered rowboat or an empty keg. As the path approached the woods, different sounds began to compete with the wildlife. Music, with percussion.

Clack. "*Pull, ye mateys, pull!*"

Clack. "*Run yon lubbers through!*"

Clack. "*Take their gold until—*"

Rollo poked his head through a thicket. "Howdy!" He tipped his hat.

The music and clacking ceased. Just inside the wood, a band of men stopped cold, like boys caught in mischief. Long hair protruded from bandannas. Every waistband sported at least one cutlass. Eye patches, hooks, and wooden legs abounded, if one can say a wooden leg abounds.

The Count pushed through the bushes and looked curiously upon the scene. Piles of logs lay around. Half finished rowboats shared the riverbank with sailboats. "Whatcha doin?" he asked.

They looked down and shuffled their feet.

"Nuthin'," a man in a blue and gold coat mumbled. He sported a black eye patch and a white-speckled shoulder.

"Wuz too! Wuz too!" squawked a brilliantly colored bird from a tree behind him.

The man spun around. "Can yer trap, snitch!"

"Can yer trap! Can yer trap! Awk!" The bird flew to a higher branch.

After admiring the bird, the Count turned to its apparent owner. "I don't recollect seein' y'all around these parts. Who are you?"

The man seemed to think hard. "Arr, a woodcutter!" He winked at the surrounding gang, and they all smiled and nodded.

"So who're these fellers then?" Rollo waved toward them.

They waved back.

"They be elves." The men nodded again and tried to look elvish.

It didn't work. Count Rollo knew better. "No, they ain't! Elves got pointy ears!"

"I crops 'em so their hats fit better."

"Makes sense," agreed the Count. "But what about them boats?" He pointed at the flotilla on the shore.

27

The leader nodded. "Ay, matey, nothing gets by ye. They be rafts to float yon logs downstream." He waved his hand toward the stacks of wood, then winced, as if he suddenly wished he hadn't.

Between the woodpiles stood his elves. In the midst of the elves stood the source of the clacking. A spoked capstan protruded from a heavy timber frame. Extending from one end of the frame was something akin to a grossly oversized wooden fork with a heavy leather sling lashed between its two tines. The fork looked like it would prefer to stand on its handle, but a taut rope from the capstan held it nearly level with the ground. A wooden catch held the capstan fast. The elves around the device stared into space and began to whistle as though they had no idea it was there.

Count Rollo had seen it, though. "What's that contraption?"

"What contraption?" The woodcutter looked around for a contraption.

Rollo pointed. "That catapult lookin' thing."

The whistling elves pivoted and stared at it in surprise.

"Oh, *that* one!" The woodcutter studied it. "Arr, it be a mousetrap."

Rollo glared at him. "Y'all think I'm a fool? Mice is little critters!"

"Rattrap."

"That's better!"

A mournful howl interrupted their conversation.

"BOOMER!" yelled Count Rollo. He loped to the end of the rattrap and looked into the sling.

An elf ran to the capstan. The Count reached into the sling and pulled out a terrified, hogtied hound. The elf hammered the catch free. The boom sprang upward in a vicious arc and crashed into a stop on the frame as soon as it was vertical. A draft swirled behind the whizzing pouch and swept Rollo's hat off his bald head, but he was too busy comforting the trembling Boomer to notice. The hat sailed through the air like a leaf.

The Count leveled accusing eyes at the woodcutter. "How'd he git in there?"

"Arr, he was after the bait."

"But he's all tied up!"

"Aye, the rats did it. They don't kindly share their booty."

"Could be. Rats is mean." Count Rollo unsheathed his dagger and cut the ropes. Boomer ran yelping back toward the castle with his tail between his legs. After the dog was gone, his master remembered his original errand. He put his knife away and turned to the woodcutter. "Y'all ain't seen no weird plant that might pop up rocks, have you?"

"Huh?" The woodcutter stood dumfounded.

"See them rocks?" The Count gestured at the lumpy line.

The woodcutter deciphered the puzzle. He nodded sagely. "Aye, matey, I knows me plants. Alee of yon rattrap stands the finest *Lobelia gihongus* I ever set me eye upon." He pointed at a plant about a foot high, with a yellow bloom. "Small it is above deck, but in the bilge it spreads fast and wide. In the Barbary Coast—er, Forest—I saw one push up a rocky shoal overnight, and it was a smaller plant than this."

"Daffodil! Daffodil!" screeched the bird behind him.

The woodcutter spun around. "Belay your beak, snitch!"

"For a cracker I will!"

"Deal."

The bird flew off.

The woodcutter again faced the Count. "Now by your leave, my elves shall destroy yon peril for ye."

"Why, sure, if y'all'd be so kind."

The elves went at it with gusto. Clubs, cutlasses, and everything else at hand was employed. Many were wounded or worse in the melee, but eventually only a bloody patch of mud remained. The plant was vanquished.

Count Rollo tried to tip his hat, but it was missing. He waved instead. The surviving elves waved back. Then he pushed back through the brush where he had come in and strolled bareheaded toward home. Halfway there, Boomer trotted up with the hat between his jaws. Rollo put the soggy thing onto his sunburned head and tossed a stick for his hound to fetch. It was a good day to be a Count.

Four

It was not such a good day down the river. Count Otto gazed out his chamber window. Pigtruffle Thicket shimmered behind heat waves rising from barren fields. The brilliant sun reflected into the Count's eyes from the undisturbed surface of the moat. Therein lay his greatest problem: the moat monster. Or rather, the absence of one.

Good monsters were hard to come by. They didn't breed often and tended to bite if anybody tried to transplant their offspring. The offspring also were snappish, which was a useful trait for edible creatures with voracious parents. One might think a young monster would express some gratitude to a Count willing to remove it from such peril, but moat monsters were notoriously ungrateful. It would not do for other Counts or the higher nobility to know that Count Otto's moat was as good for protection as a bathing pool. It had a dead mule and a few million leeches, of course, but so did most bathing pools. That partly explained the widespread aversion to baths, especially in moats.

The mule floated beneath the drawbridge. It had inflated to twice the size of the day before. That gave the Count an idea. He summoned a butler. "Send to the dungeon for the most miserable prisoner we have."

"As you wish, my lord."

Otto proceeded down the stairs to his council room. Half an hour later the Dungeon Master appeared, dragging a filthy wretch clad in tattered shreds of clothing. Scraggly hair and a long, ragged beard substituted for a tunic. Manacle sores festered about the wretch's wrists and ankles. Otto's heart ached for the poor man who had to handle such a thing.

"Release him from your grasp," he commanded. "And wash your hands."

The grateful jailer did as commanded and headed straight to the scullery.

The wretch dropped like a sack of bones.

"On your feet, wretch!"

The bones stood with an effort, but the head remained bowed.

The Count studied the wreck. "What is your name?"

"Perry the Poacher, sir, if you please."

Otto stiffened. Poaching was a capital offense. "And what did you poach, swine?"

"Oh, no, not swine, sir. Eggs. Oysters. Asparagus, sir, if you please."

The Count peered at him. "What about salmon?"

"Oh, no, sir, that would be poaching."

Perhaps two problems could be solved. Most of the kitchen staff had recently succumbed to food poisoning. That had been the theory, anyway, but now he wondered if they might have been at the wine. It did not matter; they were just as dead either way.

"Well, knave, if you were in *my* kitchen with *my* salmon, could you poach *them?*"

The prisoner thought for a minute. "Aye, sir, if you please. 'Cause then poaching wouldn't be poaching, would it, sir? If you please."

So far, so good. But almost as important as edible food was its presentation. "Can you poach a salmon, yet make it seem to swim on the platter? And can you roast a boar and yet make it look as though it is alive and angry?"

"Aye, sir! If you please, I mean."

"I do so please. But first, you must pass a test. A loyalty test.

If you pass it, you shall be released from bondage and instead shall be captain of my kitchen."

The wretch brightened. He dared to tilt his head upward a bit. "Gladly, sir! And what is the task, if you please?"

The Count leaned forward. "Tonight, by the light of the moon, you shall take to the moat in a boat…"

"Oh, no, sir!" The prisoner quailed. "Send me back to the dungeon, sir! The moat monster—"

"Fear not the monster," the Count interrupted. "You must make me a new one."

"Begging your pardon, sir?"

"Granted. But listen. In the moat floats a mule. A very dead mule. By the same arts that would make a charging boar or a swimming salmon for the table, make that mule into a monster. But you must be very careful. One wrong move, and it will explode."

"That I shall do, sir!"

"Then be off! Tell yon surly maid to find you better garb. My barber will shave you later. Take what you need to make a monster, and go!"

The Count watched Perry the Poacher stumble uncertainly in the direction of the maid. Clearly the wretch had not had much recent use of his legs. His bare, filthy feet finally intruded into her field of vision while she scrubbed and grumbled. She looked up and snarled. He backed off. She glared at the muddy footprints that followed him and snarled again. He said something to her and pointed back toward the Count. She looked balefully at the Count, arose, and headed, muttering, toward the servants' wing of the castle.

Perhaps one or two problems were on their way to resolution, thought Otto, but more than enough remained. Feeding three or four hundred people was never easy under the best of circumstances, but an understaffed kitchen made it worse. So did a general lack of food. There was the blight to

33

contend with. Locusts had not been helpful, either. To top it all off, Baron Bernie across the river had quit sending his share of the harvest to the castle. Count Otto meant to look into that.

A herald entered the council chamber. "My lord, there is a request for alms at the door."

Beggars! Just what he didn't need. "Send them to Baron Bernie! He should have plenty to spare!"

"But it is Friar Fred, my lord, soliciting for the Starving Urchins Fund."

That was different. The friars did not beg for themselves. "Send him in."

The herald left and returned momentarily with the little gray friar, who carried a little gray bag. Otto dropped a gold coin into the open sack. He grumbled, "I would rather throw in food, but we seem to have more coins than grain. And now I must feed an entire Convention of Counts who eat more than starving urchins do!"

The friar nodded his gray head. "Aye, at the Abbey we had a like problem."

"Had?"

"Had. The Abbot suggested that all bring what the Lord had graced them with and throw it into a common pot. Behold, it was awful. Raspberries and honey belong not in the same pot as rabbits and parsnips. So everybody instead brought what he had cooked of the food he was graced with, and we had better luck."

"That's it! We shall call it Pot Luck. We need not admit our grain is bad, and all will bring the best of what they have to boast. I thank you, my dear Friar. Without your help I would not have had a prayer of—" The Count stopped. He indeed would not have a prayer at the feast, food or no. He had no priest. "Er, Friar Fred, I don't suppose the Abbot could spare you for an evening, could he?"

The friar thought for a moment. "He might freely accept

other willing Counts' offerings to the Starving Urchins Fund."

"Good! Pot luck with a free will offering it will be." So Count Otto immediately sent heralds to the various counties.

The next afternoon, an ancient carriage pulled up to the mounting block. A footman leapt to the block and opened the door for an old man who held a curled metal horn to his ear. The footman helped the passenger out of the carriage while a herald jumped down from the driver's box.

The herald bowed, took the horn, lifted it to his lips, and blew a fanfare. Then he loudly announced through the same instrument: "Count Albacore the Hearing Impaired Arrives to Consult on Noble Matters with Otto, Lord of County Palindrome!"

The herald handed the trumpet back to the old Count, who put it to his ear and waited.

"Bid him in," directed Count Otto.

The first door warden relayed the order to the second door warden, who fumbled about his neck for the key.

"It's in the lock." The Count sighed.

The first door warden relayed the statement to the second door warden, who blushed and forced the creaking door open.

Otto's herald marched out the door and called, "Welcome!"

"Hah?" yelled Albacore.

The herald proceeded to the mounting block. He tilted his head upward and yelled into the trumpet, "Welcome!"

"That's better!" Count Albacore nodded and proceeded around him through the door. The second door warden shoved the groaning door shut behind him. Otto's herald ran toward the door but was too late. It was already locked.

Count Albacore strode to Count Otto. "D'ye want aught besides food at this here feast?" he yelled. "I mean, it's not that we don't got none or like we got the blight or naught like that, ye know."

Count Otto's ears rang. "Of course not!" he yelled back.

"'Cause if we did," bellowed Albacore, "we'd keep it secret, just twixt the two of us!"

"Surely!" replied Count Otto as he backed away.

Albacore followed him. "So wot else want you?"

Otto backed into the wall. He could escape no further. Then he had an idea. "How about entertainment? Perhaps a wagonload of wenches to sing?" His musicians had eloped with the most pleasant local wenches. Otto had meant to discuss that with the priest who had married them all by the light of the moon, but Father Frank was no longer available for discussions.

Albacore stared. "Ye sure?"

"Aye."

The old Count looked at him curiously and muttered in a mild fortissimo, "Well, there be no accounting for tastes, I trow. But be it as ye wish!" That having been said, he turned toward the door.

The second door warden fumbled around his neck for the key.

"It's still in the lock," groaned Count Otto.

The first door warden relayed the message to the second door warden, who blushed and twisted the key. He pulled the complaining door open, and the knocking herald fell through it. Count Albacore detoured around him, navigated to his carriage, and rode away.

Otto watched Count Albacore leave, satisfied. Everything was quiet again. Arrangements for the convention were all but complete. The castle was the cleanest it had been in two years. There would be entertainment. The food problem was resolved.

It had been a good year for wine, if not for grain. That reminded him of one last item, and he directed the butler to summon Perry. The cook arrived, wiping his floury hands on a towel.

"Poacher, I have one more command."

"Yes, my lord?"

"For the banquet, use no barrel of wine that has already been opened. Choose only the oldest, dustiest barrels. They will have aged the longest."

"Yes, my lord."

Five

"Three o'clock and all's well!" The call came at midmorning, just as the first trumpets blared to announce the earliest guests riding through the gate.

Everybody in town turned out to watch except for a disinterested sow feeding eleven piglets in the middle of the main street. She had parked there several hours before the excitement began. The sow did not know that their father would occupy a place of honor that night at the feast. Had she known, she would not have cared anyway. He had always been a male chauvinist pig.

Across the drawbridge rolled Count Albacore's ancient carriage. His banner flew proudly in the breeze, displaying two ear trumpets rampant on a field of roosters. A pair of heavy covered wagons followed him. The entourage pulled to a halt at the sow.

Count Otto peered toward the cavalcade, hoping to get a glimpse of the wenches. But no wenches appeared.

Finally the canvas opened at the back of the first wagon. Two dozen hairy men crawled out, stretched, and ambled to the other wagon. They pulled back the cover and began flinging heavy iron tools to the ground.

The Count could not decide what surprised him the most: the absence of wenches, the strange tools, or the men's costumes. All of their trousers were alike, worn uncommonly low and displaying rather more flesh in the back than he cared to see. Finally he went to Albacore's carriage and yelled through the window, "What is all this?"

"These be the wrenches ye asked for!" Albacore yelled back. "And my Plumbers' Guild to use them!"

Otto gaped. "I didn't—but—but—the entertainment!"

Albacore hobbled from the carriage. "Wait'll ye see them entertain! They practice in the Guildhall when plumbing is slow. There be not many pipes in the county, so they practice much!"

That Otto could believe. His entire county had not a single pipe unless the mad Count Eiddie the Enlightened had installed one a couple hundred years earlier. He did not mention the paucity of pipes to Count Albacore, who was parking his caravan on a side lane.

Counts continued to arrive all morning long. There was Count Barron, whose name tended to confuse seating arrangements. Count Wilbert of Wooster brought along a Gallic guest, the Marquis de Paree, who carried a tray of snails. Count Homer of Jethro. Count Jethro from Tull. Count Seymour the Sniveler. And so forth.

Countless Counts later, Count Harvey the Hunk arrived not by carriage but seated proudly astride a prancing charger. Every strand of his longish hair was in place. His muscled physique was displayed to advantage by form-fitting garb, where there was garb. Ruddy chest hair protruded proudly from the low-cut neck of his tunic. His teeth glistened, and none were missing.

Ahead of the Count marched his standard bearer, holding aloft a banner all the other counts had grown to hate. A black diagonal bar separated a powder blue field in the upper left from a hot pink field in the lower right. In each field was a single Latin word. Together with a crimson heart in the center, the coat of arms declared, "EGO ♥ FEMINI." Only the clergy could read the banner, and they declined to translate it.

Count Harvey espied a maiden in the crowd and bestowed a dazzling smile upon her. She swooned into a sighing heap of rustling fabric. He turned his head to the other side and beheld a starry-eyed housewife. Down she went. Next to go was an ancient grandmother three paces away, with her knees clicking and popping like castanets while she fell. Women were dropping like flies. There had occasionally been unkind rumors that Count Harvey employed professional swooners, but none were necessary.

Half of the birds wheeling overhead nosedived to earth. Startled townsmen ducked beneath the downy hail. Little boys scrambled to scoop up the prizes. Pigeon stew, sparrow soup, and four-and-twenty blackbird pie would be on many tables that night. The sow raised her head, spotted the Count, and flopped with a porcine smile. Behind the Count, a retinue of handsome servants administered smelling salts to the fallen, except for the sow. The air was foul with ammonia in no time. The fowl, alas, were beyond resuscitation.

Count Harvey proudly bore a platter of ladyfingers as he rode into the castle courtyard past rows of helmeted knights in polished armor. All stood at rigid attention with weapons raised and visors down. One suit of armor clattered to the ground. Harvey's smile faded.

The Captain of the Guard turned bright red.

"Deal with it later," Count Otto muttered between his teeth.

Then a commotion drew Otto's attention back to the drawbridge. Count Rollo the Clueless had arrived in—or rather on—a badly dented carriage. He was driving. His tattered banner was lashed to the brake handle. An arrow protruded from the door.

"Howdy!" called Rollo.

Suddenly the left front wheel spun off the axle and splashed into the moat ten feet below. The carriage swerved. The Count dove from the box to the center of the roadway while the battered vehicle skidded to a lopsided stop.

Count Otto hastened toward the accident.

"Dinged if it ain't just been one piece of bad luck after another!" exclaimed Count Rollo while he dusted himself off. "First the avalanche in Murderer's Gulch what squashed my flag bearer. Then the attack by highwaymen what done in my driver, and now I'm almost et by yer moat monster!" He gestured toward the remodeled mule drifting below the bridge.

Count Otto peered at the wheel-less axle hanging over the moat. "Where is your axle pin?"

"Not here, I reckon." Count Rollo shook his head.

"And what are those nicks in the axle where the pin ought to be?"

Rollo studied the axle. "Beats me. Mighta been the new groom got clumsy. He was fixin' the carriage just afore I left. Old groom keeled over from bad ale ten days ago."

"And where were the highwaymen?"

"Out by Yonder Wood. It woulda been curtains for me if a dragon hadn't taken a fancy to their leader. The rest skedaddled. So did I, truth be told."

Otto felt a swell of pride. "Aye, I hear there is a dragon there."

"A mighty fine one, I'd say," agreed Rollo. "But hold on a minute." He ducked into the wreckage of his carriage and hauled out a dented tureen.

"What's in there?" asked Otto.

"Chitlins."

A collection of blaring horns terminated the conversation. "Move it, buddy!" yelled a knight from his horse. Sirs Richard

41

the Rude and Calvin the Crude were in the service of Count Donald the Socially Unacceptable, who leaned out the window of the carriage waiting behind them. All three men and the driver were blowing horns.

"It ain't movin', see? It's broke down!" yelled Count Rollo with some heat. Sir Richard responded with a suggestion about what Count Rollo could do with his carriage. The Count reached for his scabbard, and Sir Calvin suggested what he could do with his sword.

Count Otto sighed. "Clear the bridge!"

Rollo unhitched the horses from his broken wagon and led them into town. Count Donald's knights rode back to his carriage. Gatekeepers strained at the windlass, and the drawbridge slowly pivoted upward. The broken carriage rocked forward and then tumbled end over end through the gate, stopping just short of the sow. A gang of serfs pushed the conveyance out of the road.

Finally the bridge was lowered again, and Count Donald rode sneering into town, only to find his way blocked by the sow. His driver blew his horn long and loudly, but the pig was less cooperative than Count Rollo had been. Donald finally disembarked and swaggered to the creature. He poked her with his foot and yelled to his host, "I say, Otto, be this your mother in the street?"

The indignant sow bit him and waddled off with her squealing entourage. Count Donald also squealed, but more intelligibly and less politely than the piglets.

Count Donald's knights were not present to avenge the insult to their leader. They had dismounted in the gateway and returned to the bridge to stare at the monster below them.

"An uglier creature I never did see," said Sir Richard. The creature was the color of a mule, but much rounder. A great fin that looked nearly like sailcloth extended from its back. Two bulbous eyes the size and color of watermelons protruded from the water at one end. The monster slowly turned its back to them.

"Disrespectful to knights, too!" Sir Calvin drew his bow. "Let us sting its rump as punishment." He let fly an arrow, which struck below the waterline. A jet of huge, iridescent brown bubbles squealed from the wound and floated skyward, and the monster began to move away. The knights guffawed. "Right crude he be!"

The monster accelerated, changed direction, and burbled back toward the bridge. Overhead, a curious vulture tested a bubble with its beak. A little brown cloud replaced the bubble, and the bird plummeted to the bridge.

Sir Richard's countenance changed when he beheld the buzzard at his feet and a fresh bubble floating toward him. "Away, foul vapor!" he cried and slashed the bubble with his sword.

A choking brown cloud enveloped both knights. They gagged and fell dead into the moat. The deflated monster sank. A last stream of bubbles floated heavenward.

A noisome fragrance wafted through the gate and into the town. One of Sir Albacore's plumbers sniffed the air. "Smells like work." He dug a knotted rope from the tool wagon and headed for the drawbridge.

"Aye," replied another, who opened a door to a little room in the tower to the right of the gate. He pushed past barrels of oil stockpiled for boiling in emergencies. He climbed over bags of rocks waiting to be dropped on attackers. At the back of the room, a large wooden lever extended sideways from a pivot about five feet above the floor. A chain extended upward from it to a pulley just below the ceiling, from whence it disappeared into a hole in the outer wall. A hundred beady bats' eyes stared at the plumber in inverted surprise from the bottom of the lever.

The first plumber peered into the moat. He tied one end of

43

the rope to the bridge's draw chain and threw the other end into the water. Then he pinched his nose and jumped off.

Curious townspeople edged through the gate to watch. They were rewarded a minute later by the sight of a soggy plumber climbing up the rope. A weedy chain was tied around his right ankle. He pulled himself onto the bridge and stopped long enough to remove a flopping carp that had gotten stuck halfway into the special part of his breeches. Then he untied the chain. Dragging it beside him, he returned to the gateway and sidestepped onto a foot-wide wooden ledge that projected from the front of the tower. The ledge extended from the side of the bridge to the postern gate, a dark, narrow emergency bypass around the main gate.

The plumber plucked leeches from his flesh while inspecting the stonework. Finally he spotted a rusty hook on an ancient chain, protruding from a small round hole about eight feet up and three feet to the left of the passage. Facing the tower, the plumber gripped the side of the narrow doorway with his right hand and leaned leftward. He reached up, teetered a bit, and finally managed to hang the dripping end of his chain from the hook. He released his grip on the chain and swung back into the doorway. "It be ready!" he yelled.

"Aye," hollowly replied the hole in the wall. The plumber inside the little room tugged the lever downward with both hands. Displaced bats swirled around his head. Outside the wall, the chain clanked upward.

A hideous roar erupted from the moat. Black water spiraled into a gaping chasm, carrying with it a dead mule, two suits of armor, a wagon wheel, a Viking helmet, and who knew what else.

"The moat monster!" screamed terrified spectators as they fled.

The plumber on the sill peered into the chasm.

Three levels above the hubbub, an ale and cheese reception was in progress on the castle terrace. The roar at the moat drew congregated counts from refreshment tables to the railing where they could watch the scene.

Otto glimpsed sunlight glistening from water flowing far off into the swamp and surmised where his moat water was going. The distant glimmer disappeared behind a black cloud of displaced mosquitoes.

"So I *do* have a pipe!" he said to himself.

Then he looked back at the moat and became concerned. A hollow roar continued, but not as loudly. Fresh water flowed into the moat from somewhere, but it disappeared into the hole. The moat did not refill. Fish flip-flopped amidst remaining debris. Several other Counts had also noticed and seemed to be making mental notes.

The first plumber tilted his head toward the hole in the wall. "Jiggle yon handle!" he yelled.

"Aye," replied the hole. The chain bounced up and down, and the roaring ceased. The moat refilled with a hissing noise. The plumber sidestepped on the narrow ledge to the bridge.

Disappointed Counts returned to the food tables.

Otto's eye was caught by a sparkle from the river. There was an unusual eddy in the middle of the channel. *I have* two *pipes!* he thought triumphantly.

Six

The courtyard below was nearly empty. Servants, who had been banned from there during the procession of Counts, were now inside the castle serving the same Counts. All standing knights had trooped off after the last of the guests had entered.

One prone suit of armor remained on the floor. It moved. An arm creaked toward the latch that secured the breastplate to the back. The latch would not budge when the iron gauntlet scraped across it.

"Most knights remove their gloves first," the Captain of the Guard said from the corner, where he stood, watching. He had stayed behind. The iron arm fell back to the flagstones and did not move.

The disgusted captain approached the heap. "Well, then, I must help, though I do not wish to." With the point of his sword, he undid the latch and swung the hinged breastplate open to reveal women's clothing. He drew back in surprise; the armor clanged shut. "Ugh! 'Tis worse than I had imagined! To swoon for a man during review is bad enough, but to garb oneself as a woman…"

"And how *should* a woman garb herself?" retorted the armor.

The captain stared. Iron hands removed an iron helmet to reveal the iron visage of the surly maid at her surliest. She flung off the gauntlets, yanked the breastplate open, and began to wriggle out of the armor.

"*If* you please, sir, you will allow a lady to undress in

privacy!"

The captain obligingly faced the other direction. While metal clattered behind him, he wondered if a surly maid was technically a lady, and whether a woman in armor was much of a lady either. He had not yet reached a conclusion before the clattering was replaced by bare feet slapping across the courtyard. He whirled and drew his sword but was too late as her skirts swirled around the corner. While he sheathed his weapon, he wondered how she could have fit into a suit of armor while wearing a skirt. He would ask his wife that night. No, he had better not. For that matter, he had better just tell the Count that the swooning knight had been dealt with, not that she had gotten away while his back was turned.

The convention convened after the reception. Counts dispersed to various working sessions as they were announced by Turner, the Page. "The Blight Problem" was cancelled due to lack of attendance. Nobody would admit to having a blight problem. "Enhanced Techniques in Grain Trade Revenue Generation" was also a dud until Turner rechristened it "More Corn for the Count," after which it had to be moved to a larger hall. Counts with a scientific bent could discuss "The Philosopher's Stone: Fact or Fiction?" More practical ones dealt with serf maintenance, dealing with unruly barons, and so forth. Some attendees, though, only studied the food tables and audited the ale.

The sun dipped toward the horizon. "Dinner is served!" Turner finally announced.

Most of the Counts trooped into the main hall. Some

stumbled in. Servants showed them all to their assigned seats. There was some grumbling among Counts who felt snubbed due to their distance from the head table, but Perry the Poacher had arranged for those at the farthest tables to be first in the serving line. They could not grumble effectively with their mouths full. The more highly honored guests dared not complain.

Count Otto arose. The noise did not abate. He tapped his goblet several times with his knife. No change. He turned and nodded to a knight standing behind him. The knight clanked to the middle of the hall, swung a mace over his head, and shattered a serving table. Silence ensued. Otto nodded, and the knight clanked back to his post.

"Thank you. Friar Fred will offer the blessing."

The surprised assemblage stared with some hostility when the little gray man arose. They had expected their rank to be worth at least a full-fledged priest or maybe a junior-grade bishop, but all the Count had gotten for them was a friar. Not even the Abbot. They arose nonetheless for the prayer and sat down immediately afterward. There was only grumbling instead of the usual bedlam while the diners speared the first round of dainties.

Then Count Donald called out, "Hey, Otto, why'd you bring us only a friar? Couldn't you afford a priest? You been excommunicated or something?" He guffawed.

Count Otto savored the moment. "Nay, my friend. Alas, Father Frank, my priest of high esteem, was devoured by a dragon not a fortnight ago, may God rest his soul."

"Amen," responded the crowd while they chewed.

Then he played his ace card. "Not by just any dragon, though. But by one in Yonder Wood, in *my* county, and by all accounts one of the finest dragons."

Count Donald spewed mead out his nose. He set down his tankard and laughed raucously. *"Finest* dragons? In *this* flea-bitten county? Pshaw! More likely the priest was scared to death by a salamander!"

"I *beg* your pardon!" boomed a voice from a window high in the wall, followed by a blast of flame.

Count Donald instantly became a charred, smoking heap. His sword clattered to the floor in a room that had otherwise gone deathly quiet. Everybody gaped at the remains of Count Donald and then looked up.

A long, red neck extended through the window. A double row of jagged spines like saws' teeth ran along its top. Up near the chandelier, the neck connected to an enormous ruddy head plated with scales. Two bright yellow eyes glowed with anger. Two huge nostrils emitted pulses of smoke every time the creature exhaled. A forked tongue slid out of the giant mouth and tested the air. The eyes relaxed slightly.

"Please pardon my interruption." The dragon surveyed the room. It sniffed at the tendril of smoke wafting from Count Donald and looked at Count Otto. "May I?"

"Be my guest," answered the Count. He wondered what else he could say to a dragon under such circumstances.

"Thank you." More neck came through the window as the dragon bent its head toward the table. Both forks of its tongue embraced the carboniferous Count Donald, conveyed him to the open mouth, and uncoiled. The dragon swallowed. The crowd sat mesmerized, watching a lump move up the neck like a rabbit in a snake. The dragon lapped up the mead from the late Count's tankard. It took quite a while because forked tongues are hard to lap with.

After the dragon had finished, it lifted the fallen sword by the hilt with one fork of its tongue, picked its teeth, and laid the sword on the table. Then it daintily wiped its mouth on a banner hanging from the wall and withdrew.

When the last puff of smoke dissipated, people began to whisper. Finally one Count said in a subdued voice, "That's the finest dragon I ever saw!"

"And a real gentleman too!" responded another. "It didn't even scorch the tablecloth!"

Count Otto beamed. "More food!" he called. Dining resumed in earnest. So did noise.

Over the hubbub arose a short scream, followed by unhealthy choking and gurgling. A blue-faced servant clutched at his throat and crumpled to the ground by Count Rollo's chair.

"Dang!" the Count expostulated. "That's the fourth taster this week!"

Staring neighbors edged away from him.

Rollo looked sadly at his plate. "Must be sumpin' he et." He surveyed the room. Everybody else's taster was still standing. "Hmm! Must be just me. Hey, Otto!" he yelled. "Got any extra vittles?"

"Take Donald's!" Otto called back. "He's done."

"*Well* done, ye mean," muttered Rollo as he sent a servant around the table. "Just so long as I don't get his obnoxiousness too, rest his rotten little soul."

Finally the meal was finished, except for six or seven desserts and eight or nine barrels of wine. Nobody had touched Count Caspar's broccoli casserole. Counts don't have to eat broccoli. Caspar had tried to explain this to Countess Fern, but she had insisted. "Vegetables are better for you," she had said. Caspar didn't eat the casserole either but finished a third helping of boar to make up for it. He'd chew a little parsley before returning home so Fern wouldn't know.

A few extemporaneous duels had occurred during dinner. Most were nonfatal, but the diners had enjoyed them anyway. It finally was time for real entertainment. Count Otto clapped his hands twice. A curtain opened at the end of the hall to reveal Count Albacore's band of plumbers with wrenches in their hands. Several recorders, two krummhorns, a shawm, and a bevy of sackbuts blasted a nasal fanfare, and the musicale began:

> "Behold, we lusty plombres be
> A'carving pypes from hollow tree
> To brynge ye water from far hylle
> To sprynging font nigh wyndowsylle.
> Hey, nonny nonny,
> Spurt and spraye,
> Aye, rilly nilly,
> Drippe, drippe, away!"

At the last line of the chorus, all plumbers but one spun clockwise away from the audience and bowed to more clearly display the costume of their guild. The other one pivoted counterclockwise and was instantly replaced by a flash of flame and a puff of smoke.

"A little more care for the choreography, please," said the dragon from the upper window. The dancing improved.

> "We carve yon channel from yon brooke
> And bury pipe no more to looke
> At from inside thy cot or hall
> Until it poppeth through thy wall."

Another flash, another puff, and one less plumber. "Third tenor, a semihemidemitone sharp." The singing improved.

> "Hey, nonny nonny,
> Spurt and spraye,
> Aye, rilly nilly,
> Drippe, drippe, away!
> We fyxxe thy leaking water line
> To house for man or stall for kine,

*And if ye wish, e'en nae a creeke,
Thou mayest bathe most every weeke!
Hey, nonny nonny,
Spurt and spraye,
Aye, rilly nilly,
Drippe, drippe, away!
And when thou finishest thy drynke
And watch it gurgle down the synke,
Our plombynge will transport it till
It run to earth and ye get our bylle!
Hey, nonny nonny,
Spurt and spraye,
Aye, rilly nilly,
Drippe, drippe, away!"*

The Counts cheered and whistled. All remaining functional plumbers faced the audience, bowed, and immediately commenced an intricate juggling routine. Back and forth flew wrenches until somebody stumbled over a spanner.

Flash! Puff!

The juggling improved. Then as a grand finale, all the plumbers flung their twirling tools into the air over the middle of the stage. Wrenches interlocked amidst wild clanging to form a four-sided tower, wide at the base and tapering to a point just below the ceiling.

The Marquis de Paree leapt to his feet. "Alors!" he yelled. "I have a vision for a great tower in mon Citee!"

"Pay him no mind," whispered Count Wilbert to Otto. "He always has visions."

Amidst wild applause, the surviving plumbers picked up their wrenches and trooped off the stage. The dragon cleaned up the residue. Count Albacore beamed while other Counts deluged him with service requests.

Suddenly there was a crash. A full wine barrel had toppled

from a balcony onto Count Rollo's chair. Everything within twenty feet of the smashed furniture was purple. Fortunately for the Count, he had just left his seat to see about hiring a plumber. He stooped to the floor, dipped his fingers into a puddle, and tasted. "Good stuff, this. What a waste! Oughta store vinegar up there an' wine in the cellar, not t'other way."

The convention was finally over. "Eight o'clock and all's well!" wafted through the window. It had not really been eight o'clock for some time, but the assessment was otherwise correct. All surviving guests had either sloshed out the doorway or collapsed in the corners. Very few had fallen into the moat.

Count Otto happily surveyed the wreckage. It had been a good party.

The dragon poked its head through the window and purred smokily. "Excellent feast, my good Count! I really couldn't eat another plumber!"

Seven

Otto arose full of resolution three days later. It had taken awhile to get over the feast. The time had come to fix some problems, not the least of which was the land across the river. Baron Bernie and his serfs were seriously behind schedule on their grain taxes. The speaker in the taxation session had warned against letting such things slide.

There also was no priest to pray for deliverance from the locusts and the blight. Father Frank had preached about locusts once, famines several times, and miraculous food a time or two besides. He had even preached about greedy farmers. But the priest was dead, and the bishop was in no apparent rush to replace him. Otto decided to borrow a friar.

The Abbey was only five miles away but was not subject to the Count. Neither was it directly beholden to the Bishop. Itinerant monks had evangelized the populace years before the Church formally established itself in the land. Costello the Abbot was an authority in his own right, and he might object to a nobleman trying to appropriate one of his friars. Otto needed to make a good impression.

"Have my chamberlain bring me fresh raiment," he ordered the nearest servant.

The servant looked curiously at him. "But my Lord, you had the chamberlain beheaded eleven days ago."

The Count goggled. "I did?"

"Aye, my Lord."

"For what reason?"

"Begging your pardon, my Lord, but I know not. The Chief

Steward commanded it in thy name."

"But I—I...so be it. His head cannot be restored. You are my new chamberlain."

The man turned pale.

"And you will answer to me, not to the Chief Steward."

The brevet chamberlain returned to normal color and hustled away for fresh clothing.

Otto nodded at another servant. "You, summon my barber."

The man looked confused. "But my Lord, you had him discharged four days ago."

"And why did I do that?"

"You said nobody should hold a sharpened razor to your throat."

A glimmer of suspicion arose. "And where was I when I spake so?"

"I know not, my Lord. The Chief Steward from the dungeon said..."

"The Chief Steward lies!" shouted the Count. "Find me my barber!" The startled servant ran off.

The Count faced the next servant. "I see I have some business with the Chief Steward this morning. But this afternoon, I must be off to the Abbey. Have my horse saddled and ready to go at two o'clock."

"Begging your pardon, my Lord, but..."

The Count gripped the arms of his chair so tightly his fingers turned white. "I *do* have a horse yet, do I not?"

"Yea, my Lord," stammered the servant. "A plow horse for which you traded last week. The Chief Steward..."

"Shall lose his head!" the Count roared, leaping from his seat. He rumbled down the dark back hall, down the steep stairs, past the silent wine cellar, to the dungeon door. "Headsman, I have need of you!"

The headsman rose from his chair. His arm was in a sling

55

and a bandage was wrapped around his neck. "I am sorry, my Lord, but I am not fit. Not since you commanded me to cut my own head off."

The Count pounded the table. Checkers rattled to the floor. "I *what?*"

"The Chief Steward said you ordered me to."

"And you *tried?*"

"Aye, my Lord, but it was hard. I twisted my arm. Shall I try again now, or wait until I am healed?"

"Neither. I ordered no such thing." The Count picked up a gore-encrusted axe. "But *I* shall try with the Chief Steward's head! Take me to him!"

The undamaged Dungeon Master lifted the bar and pulled the door open. He took the lantern and preceded the Count down the stairs. At the first door on the left he pulled out his great key and inserted it into the lock.

No sooner had the lock rattled than a wail arose from inside the cell. The Dungeon Master looked wide-eyed at the Count, who gripped the axe tighter and nodded. The Dungeon Master twisted the key and pulled at the door. The wail crescendoed to a scream, then wavered into slobbering sobs.

A powerful stench of rotten food, stale wine, and human waste swirled out of the cell. The only light came from the lantern. The hole by the ceiling was dark. Beneath it, the Chief Steward clawed and licked at the wall. The slippery floor was littered with broken glass. He turned. His face was purple and bloody. Wild, dilated eyes reflected the flame of the lamp. He spun back, screaming with greater vigor, and clawed at the wall. His visitors retreated with their hands over their ears. The Dungeon Master slammed the cell door shut. The echoing boom nearly deafened the two men. They wished it had.

The prisoner stopped screaming only long enough to catch a shuddering breath. No sooner did the door close than his howling redoubled. The Dungeon Master and the Count dashed back up the stairs and pounded to be let out. The headsman finally pulled the door open with his good arm. The white-faced men raced through and shoved it shut behind them. They could not fully shut in the wailing, though.

"The prisoner yet has his head," observed the damaged headsman.

The Count set down the axe. "No, he has lost it. It would be a mercy to kill him, and he deserves none." He headed shakily up the passageway. His ears rang.

Otto was still shaking by the time he reached the door of the wine cellar. Maybe a drink would calm him. He stepped inside and hung his lamp on a hook. He grabbed the nearest flagon and filled it from the dusty barrel he had recently tapped. For testing, of course. The Count took a deep swallow just as he realized that the flagon might contain old poison. He waited. Nothing bad seemed to be happening, but dilution might be in order just in case. Obviously any drinking ware in the cellar was out. He poured some wine into his hand. Too slow. He might be dying at that very moment! There was no time to waste! He leaned backward beneath the tap, gripped the spigot between his jaws, and opened the valve.

Wine poured down his throat, gagging him. Wine flowed down his windpipe, choking him. Wine spurted out of his mouth and into his eyes. They burned. The spluttering Count let go of the spout with his teeth. *Bad move,* he thought and fell backward onto the floor. His shoulders mostly broke the fall. His head only made a small splashy thump in the growing puddle of wine.

He stumbled to his feet and dared to open a stinging eye long enough to find the valve. He shut both the valve and the eye. He staggered toward where he thought the table should be, with his hand flailing before him. Finally he stumbled into it. The remaining goblets careened to the floor. The Count leaned heavily upon the table with both hands and waited for the world around him to slow its spinning.

Suddenly he remembered his two o'clock appointment with a horse. He arose from the table, reeling slightly, retrieved his lamp, and stumbled from the room. The passageway seemed to have gotten longer while he was away, and somebody must have added a few more steps in the stair to the main floor.

Eventually he wobbled back into the great hall.

The new chamberlain stood by the Count's chair with a full set of clean clothing. He froze as the Count approached.

"Well, don't just stand there staring. Dress me!" commanded the Count.

"Y-yes, my lord," replied the servant, and did so.

"Why is my barber not yet here?"

"He is coming, my lord, but they had to find him first."

"Where was he?"

"In a butcher's stall, sir, slaughtering pigs." The barber rushed in at that moment, wiping his razor on his breeches. Count Otto sagged into his chair. His throat began to hurt.

The barber stared, dumfounded, at the Count.

"Well," the Count demanded impatiently, "which do you prefer: barbering or butchery?"

"Barbering, my lord. It's quieter."

"Then shave me. But do not forget which trade you are following when you do it."

"No, my lord. I mean, yes, my lord. I mean..."

"Never mind, just shave."

No sooner had the barber finished than another wide-eyed servant approached. "My lord, your steed awaits."

"Good!" The Count stood up. His brain orbited a time or two and finally decided to go with him. He proceeded, brain and all, out the castle entrance to the mounting block. Then he stopped. Never before had he seen his fancy saddle cinched to a swaybacked nag with blinders. Flies swirled around its head. The steed was chewing a mouthful of hay. It scratched its belly with a hind knee.

"Am I a serf? Remove those blinders!" demanded the Count.

"Begging your pardon, my lord, but…," began the groom.

"I wish to look like a Count!"

The groom looked doubtfully at him. "As you say." No sooner was the deed done than the horse glared at its owner. The owner glared back. The horse swallowed the rest of its hay. The Count stepped into the stirrup. The nag tore away a piece of his sleeve with long yellow teeth and chewed some more.

"If you will mount from the other side, my lord, she will not see you," the groom offered.

Otto transferred his glare from the horse to the groom. "Do you mean—?"

"Aye, my lord. She is blind in the right eye."

"Then why did—?"

"But, my Lord, the Chief Steward said—"

"Say no more," sighed the Count. He mounted from the opposite side and spurred the horse forward. It walked in a circle to the left. He tugged the reins to the right. It still veered to port, but in a larger circle. "Will it not walk straight?" he yelled at the groom.

"With the blinders she will, sir."

He drew the beast to a halt on its next circuit past the mounting block. "Install them."

The groom put on the blinders from the right side. The Count applied the spurs. The nag snorted and proceeded at a good plowing pace.

"At this rate I should be at the Abbey by next week," Otto grumbled.

An hour later and halfway to his destination, the Count approached a gaggle of serfs in a field. He hid his torn sleeve against his side. He sucked in his stomach and tried to reallocate the displaced poundage to his chest. Staring men tightly gripped their spades. Gaping children ran screaming to hide behind their mothers' skirts. The mothers looked like hens sheltering chicks from a hawk.

I must inspire awe, Otto thought and inhaled deeply to expand his chest. A swirling fly was drawn into his nose, and he sneezed violently. When his chest returned to its usual location, the horse stopped from the shift in cargo. The stunned fly spiraled to the ground.

"God bless you," murmured the serfs.

"Thank you." The Count wiped his nose with his bad sleeve. Then he spied a familiar face just off the road in front. So did his ride. It threw the Count and ran whinnying to nuzzle a grimy farmer. The farmer reached for the horse but stopped and looked in fear at his lord.

The Count pulled himself to his feet. He was still fully assembled if the aches meant anything. "Be this your horse?"

The man went pale. He stammered, "N-n-nay, sir, but it was once. Until your Lordship traded, I mean." He indicated a fine-looking stallion behind him, tied to a plow.

"Do you not care for my—your—horse you have now?"

The serf searched for words, as if he feared they might be his last. "Well, my lord, begging your pardon, sir, but the horse that *was* yours knows not how to plow."

"Well, then, I command you to trade it back. We must not have a farmer that cannot plow."

"Bless you, sir!" exclaimed the farmer. He hastily transferred the saddle to the stallion and helped the Count aboard with muddy hands.

As the peasants watched the Count depart, the first farmer turned to his neighbor. "He ain't too bad for a nobleman, even if he do decorate himself strangely."

The neighbor nodded. "No accounting for Counts' tastes. Mayhap it wards off robbers when he rides alone."

Now that he was back on his stallion, Count Otto's travel speed improved considerably, and the serfs receded into the background. Soon he rode between healthy green fields. Gray robed, hooded forms resembling overgrown mushrooms raised their faces and crossed themselves as he passed, after which they bowed again to their hoeing.

The Count was in foreign territory. He had no formal authority on abbey grounds. After dismounting by the doorway, he tied his horse to a post and entered the building.

A friar at a table looked up, jolted in surprise, and crossed himself. "Welcome to the Abbey. May I help you?"

"I wish to speak with the Abbot Costello."

"Please hold." The friar ducked through an arched doorway and returned a minute later. "I am sorry. The Abbot is either away from his cell or engaged in other business, but your visit is very important to us. Please take a form from Pile 1 if you wish to join, Pile 2 for prayer, Pile 3 for shelter, Pile 4 for alms, Pile 5 for hot cross buns, Pile 6 for Abbey wine, Pile 7 for illumination of texts, Pile 8 for today's theological joke, Pile 9 for an oath of chastity, or Pile Zero for all other requests." He smiled.

Count Otto could not read. He looked helplessly at the piles. All of the forms looked confusing except for the ones in Pile Zero. They were blank sheets. He picked one up and carried it back to the friar. "How do I—-?"

The friar took the parchment from him. "Thank you. Please step this way." He led the Count into another chamber populated by another friar. The first friar crossed himself and left.

The second friar's eyebrows lifted nearly to his tonsured hairline. He crossed himself and arose. "Welcome to the Abbey, where our mission statement is 'Your soul is our burden.' For medical care, please take a form from Pile 1. For a cup of cold water, Pile 2. To borrow a friar, Pile 3. For—."

The count reached for Pile 3, but it was empty. "I am sorry," recited the friar. "That pile is temporarily out of service. Please hold for assistance. While you are waiting, you may select inspirational sounds of your choice. For Aberdonian melodies, please take a form from Pile 8. For our very own Gregory Brothers, Pile 9." He withdrew from the room.

Otto wondered where Aberdonia might be and picked up a sheet from Pile 8. He dropped it when a bagpipe began to bleat behind him. The piper stifled his pipes and faded back into the shadows. The Count lifted a leaf from Pile 9. Four neatly tonsured monks with handlebar mustaches stepped from an alcove and commenced chanting in harmony.

Two and a half chants later, the Abbot entered the room. The monks backed into their alcove, still singing. The Abbot glided to the wall and rotated a knob counterclockwise. The singing subsided to a hum. He tweaked it a bit to the right. The hum became slightly louder. Satisfied, the Abbot nodded and turned to Otto. "How may I help you?"

"I would like to borrow a friar."

"Ah, yes, Option 3B. For what purpose?"

"I lack a priest, and the Bishop seems in no hurry to send a new one."

The Abbot looked the Count up and down. He particularly inspected the face. "Perhaps he has too few to cast them all to dragons. I would choose to know why you come requesting a friar when your face is as purple as a Pict's. You've not taken up Druidism, have you?"

Otto raised his wine-stained hands to protest. Then he understood why everybody had stared at him so oddly. Awe was not what he inspired. "Nay. I had an accident with a barrel."

"Indeed. I take it the barrel bled to death. But back to business. The Counts were generous with their gold for the Starving Urchins Fund, and the urchins also enjoyed the leftovers you sent. Except for the broccoli casserole. I shall send Friar Fred your way as soon as he returns from fishing with the Rabbi." Noting the curious look on the Count's face, the Abbot explained. "Option 8A, you know."

"Oh, yes. Thank you."

"We are always happy to help."

Otto paused. "Then perhaps you may help me with another problem. I recall a sermon about serfs who would not pay their lord his grain allotment. My subjects across the river do exactly that. Would it be Christian to kill them? And their Baron as well?"

63

The Abbot shook his head. "Nay, they are not the problem. The pirates prevent their passage."

"Pirates?"

"Aye, on the river."

"We shall see about that!" the Count rumbled.

The Abbot raised his hand. "You came alone. I will send MacGregor the Monk with you."

"What could a monk do?"

"You shall see." The Abbot lifted a paper from Pile 8. Immediately a fearsome-looking monk with a gray plaid robe, great red beard, and tonsured red hair stumped into the room. He carried a hoe and a bagpipe. A foul-looking sack was slung over his shoulder. Setting the hoe against the wall, he placed the pipe to his lips and began to inflate the bag until the Abbot stopped him. "No music, please. You would clash with the Gregory Brothers."

The plaid monk glowered as the bag hissed flat. "Why then did ye call me, Father-r-r-r? I was doing war-r-r-r with the r-r-r-rabbits."

"You shall accompany the Count on the river road as he approaches the pirates' lair."

MacGregor's eyes glinted. "Ahh! They be mor-r-r-re of a challenge than r-r-r-rabbits!"

"Have a care, brother," warned the Abbot. "Forget not that you are a man of peace."

"Aye. I shall only play my pipes and pr-r-r-ractice my swing. Come, Count!" he ordered and shouldered the hoe. They reretraced Otto's steps through the antechambers. Before they reached the exit, the friar in the inner chamber hastened to the Count.

"Would you care to fill out a questionnaire on our service?" He thrust a form into the Count's left hand and a quill pen into his right. The paper had two square boxes: one very large with bold writing next to it, and a very small one with tiny writing.

Otto had never held a pen before. "What do I do?"

"Draw an 'X' in one box, from corner to corner." Otto decided to try the larger box. It gave him more room to work. He scratched a shaky "X" and handed the form back. "Thank you," said the friar. "Your feedback is always appreciated."

"Have a nice day!" called the second friar as they passed through his antechamber.

"What did the writing say by the box I marked?" asked Otto while MacGregor the Monk helped him into the saddle.

"Exemplar-r-r-ry ser-r-r-rvice."

"And by the other?"

"In need of impr-r-r-rovement."

They traveled in silence for some time. Suddenly the monk stopped. He leaned his hoe against the horse. Staring fixedly into the field to their right, he reached into a pocket of his robe and drew out a round stone about the size of a hen's egg. He laid it on the road and retrieved the hoe.

"What are you doing?" asked Otto.

"Shh!" whispered MacGregor. "A r-r-r-rabbit!" He gripped the hoe with both hands and raised it over his head. Then he swiftly swung it in a clockwise arc and whacked the stone, which sailed through the air and landed with a plop. The monk hurried into the field. Curious, Otto followed.

A dead rabbit lay beneath the stone. The monk took his hoe and tapped the stone into a nearby hole, recently inhabited by a rabbit. Striding to the hole, he reached in and retrieved his missile. He dropped stone and quarry into his pocket. A smile cracked his beard. "Bunny pie tonight!"

"What do you call this weapon?" asked the Count.

"Flog."

They returned to the road. Shortly afterward, they reached a crossing by a ruined inn. Straight ahead would take them back to the castle. The left fork led to Yonder Wood. That lane was looking a bit weedy since the dragon had taken up residence.

The right fork had seen even less travel recently. Grass sprouted in the tracks. Toads and mosquitoes played undisturbed in water-filled ruts. This was the road to the river crossing.

The travelers turned right. For several minutes, all was silent but the splash of retreating toads and the hum of attacking mosquitoes. Then other sounds arose.

"Arrrr!"

"Avast!"

"Hardtack *again?*"

The road rounded a last bend, and the river came into view. It was about a hundred yards wide and flowed slowly from left to right. An arched stone bridge spanned it immediately ahead. Fifty yards upstream from the bridge, a rock approximately eight feet across and four feet high jutted from the middle of the river. Ten men jostled for space on the tiny island. Others sat in a flotilla of rowboats anchored around it.

"Ye bilge swillin', scupper swallowin' wharf rat, getcher stinkin' hook off me grog barrel!" One pirate on the rock pushed another.

"Will not!"

A scuffle ensued, and the first pirate fell off with a splash. Immediately something streaked through the water toward him, leaving a V-shaped wake behind it. The water bubbled and roiled. A great green tail with a spade-shaped end flipped from the surface some thirty feet away and disappeared. All was quiet.

"Greenie got ol' Deadeye."

"Arr."

"More grog for the rest of us now."

"Aye."

"Ahoy! Bounty ashore!" A pirate had sighted Count, monk, and horse. Five boats disembarked from the rock. Each held from three to eight men, all armed to the teeth—literally, since they clutched daggers between their jaws.

"Fire across their bows!" A dagger clattered from the mouth of their captain. A pirate launched a flaming arrow. A V-shaped wake sped ahead of the boats. A monstrous green head atop a long green neck shot from the water and grabbed the arrow between its teeth. It reversed course and swam back toward the boats with the flaming arrow held aloft.

"No, Greenie, don't fetch!" screamed the pirates. Daggers clattered. "Bad serpent! Bad serpent!" But Greenie wasn't listening. He dropped the arrow into a pile of coiled, oily rope in the closest boat. Black smoke was followed by a burst of flames. The serpent's tongue lolled from the side of his mouth, and his tail wagged happily in the air thirty feet behind him. Pirates dove from the flaming vessel, and Greenie gobbled them up. His tail wagged faster. Then he disappeared.

The surviving boats resumed their approach. Count Otto steered his horse behind a tree. MacGregor the Monk remained in the open. He drew a stone from his pocket. Setting it on the ground, he squatted and sighted with the hoe. He arose, licked his finger, and tested the breeze. He prepared to swing.

Count Otto crouched in the brambles. A thorn raked his knuckles. "How many boats are coming?"

"FOUR-R-R-R!" A whoosh and a clack on shore were shortly followed by a plop, a scream, and a clatter from the nearest boat. A pirate with a misshapen forehead collapsed. His companions dived to the floorboards to avoid MacGregor's attention. They should have remembered to drop their daggers first. The boat drifted off, carrying wailing pirates toward Deadly Falls a mile downstream. Men in the three remaining boats were made of sterner stuff, though. They continued their assault.

The monk bowed his head for a moment. "I dinna wish it to come to this," he said as he swung the sack from his shoulder. From it he drew an evil-looking bagpipe. The bag was unadorned by any cover, as naked as the day it was dragged out of some animal. Gnarled pipes of briar protruded from it in various directions. Some had thorns. The crooked mouthpiece disappeared into the monk's beard. He took a deep breath and blew. The bag inflated. He squeezed it beneath his arm. A squawk like a wounded duck issued from one pipe and was shortly followed by something like the tormented souls of a thousand sheep.

"NO, NOT THAT!" screamed the pirates. More daggers clattered.

"THE ABERDONIAN BLADDER OF DEATH!" The boats raced back to the rock. Meanwhile, three huge green heads popped from the water and listened intently. Tears streamed from their eyes.

"AAULLD," howled the nearest.

"LAAANNG," moaned the second.

"SYYYYNNNE," droned the last.

All three dove from sight. The song, if it could be called that, ended shortly afterward. MacGregor the Monk withdrew the tube from his mouth. The bag hissed flat, filling the air with a rancid odor. The monk stowed his pipes, picked up his hoe, and turned from the river.

Count Otto watched with disbelief. "Will you not use your weapons to drive the pirates from their island?"

"Nay, I am a man of peace."

"You say that after braining a man with a flog?"

"I war-r-r-rned him. He dinna duck."

They started back, preceded by frogs and escorted by mosquitoes. The Count broke the quiet. "Your Bladder of Death—what is it?"

"Bar-r-nar-r-r-rd."

"I beg your pardon?"

"'Tis Bar-r-nar-r-r-rd. 'Twas Bar-r-nar-r-r-rd from whence I took it. 'I will be Bar-r-nar-r-r-rd until it r-r-rots."

68

"Who—or what—was Barnard?"

"A fell beast, it was." The monk scowled at the memory. "Akin to a lizar-r-r-rd, I ween, but of gr-r-r-reat size and the color-r-r-r of lilacs. 'Twould sing and dance on its hind legs to entice tender-r bair-r-r-rns into its lair-r-r-r." His visage darkened. "Then 'twould suck out their br-r-r-rains."

"How foul! Would they not cry out?"

"Nay. They smiled."

The Count shivered. "How did you vanquish it?"

"I cr-r-r-rouched outside its hole and cackled like a babe. The Bar-r-nar-r-r-rd danced through the door-r-r-r, singing, 'I love you!' Then I flogged it." He shook his head. "But let us speak no mor-r-r-re of such things and consider-r-r-r fair-r-r-rer ones instead."

They reached the fork in the road. The monk turned left and the count turned right.

One thought of rabbit pie.

The other considered ways to rid the river of pirates.

It was settled that Friar Fred would stay nights at the castle instead of commuting from the Abbey, by order of the Abbot. "I do not intend to supply midnight snacks for dragons," the Abbot had said.

So that first night, the friar said his prayers and curled up in a corner near the fire. He pulled his hood over his face and slept...well, actually, he overslept.

It was nearly five in the morning when footsteps awakened him. The friar slid his hood back in the dark and watched. It was only Perry the Poacher, headed to the kitchen to start breakfast for the castle. Clattering and scraping ensued as fresh wood was laid in the great cooking fireplace and coals were coaxed back to life. Squawking from the henhouse outside indicated that somebody else was already collecting eggs.

Friar Fred knelt and said his morning prayers. He added an apology to his Lord for being behind schedule. Such a prayer was not included in the breviary, but he felt it was appropriate. Then he arose and headed toward the kitchen. A nice mug of something hot would be welcome.

Perry was poking at the fire. As flames began to illuminate the kitchen, he turned and saw the friar. "Good day, Father!"

Friar Fred smiled and shook his head. "I shall never be a father, only a brother."

Perry seemed disappointed. "Oh, I thought…"

The friar waited, but there was silence. Finally he said, "But if you need a father, a father shall I be to you. Would it be for confession, perhaps?"

"Aye."

"No confessional have I, but your words will be sealed." A fresh squawk came through the outside door. "Shall we find a place where we will not be troubled by people with eggs?"

Perry nodded. He led the friar across the service passage to a storeroom full of cabbages and closed the door.

Silence. Darkness. The poacher cleared his throat. "The Chief Steward was an evil man."

"So are we all."

"It was the Chief Steward's desire that the Count would be overthrown."

"But why?"

"Methinks he served a different master."

"Many men do."

"I meant…yes, yes, I understand. But why does God allow such things?"

The friar thought for a minute. "You asked me a question,

so I will ask you one. When God served Jonah to a fish, did the fish know it served God?"

"I don't know."

"Neither do I. Only God knows. Please continue."

"The Steward's commands for preparation of the feast were sure to make it fail. Some men would die. The Count would be disgraced at best and murdered at worst."

"That is a strong accusation. Have you proof?"

"Indeed. The Chief Steward bade that a barrel of wine should be carried to the balcony, to be ready at need. Four men it took to carry it thence from the cellar."

"The barrel that fell onto Count Rollo's chair?"

"The same."

"But who pushed it?"

"The Chief Steward."

Friar Fred shook his head in the dark. "That cannot be! He was a prisoner in the dungeon!"

"Yea, and nay. He had a key to his own cell."

"How do you know this?"

"When one is in the dark and quiet of a dungeon, one hears every sound and sees every light because any of them might spell either freedom or the end. Or both. Be that as it may, I would often hear a key in the Chief Steward's lock when no jailer was about. Often would I hear him creep down the hall, push open a panel in the ceiling, and pull himself up." Just as often would I later hear him drop back down, pull the panel into place, and return to his cell. Then I would hear the click of his lock."

"But I saw no panel!"

"Did you look for one?"

The friar thought. "Nay."

"The ceiling is uneven, and the dungeon is dark."

"True. But what is above the hole?"

"The wine cellar. The hole is in a corner behind the

barrels."

"How do you know this?"

"I would hear rats singing when he opened it. Then the night of the feast, I thought I saw him in a shadow on the balcony above the great hall. Surely enough, he crept behind the barrel I told you about, and pushed. Then he crept back into the shadow. So as soon as the feast was over, I descended the ladder from the kitchen into the wine cellar and closed the cover in the ceiling behind me. But the hole in the floor was open! I took my torch and climbed back into the dungeon I had hoped never to see again. The Chief Steward's cell door was standing ajar. I crept in and looked about. The lock would latch as soon as the door was pulled shut, but there were keyholes on both sides. Hidden beneath The Chief Steward's pallet was a great key, too big to carry easily while creeping about a castle. Then I sinned, Father—er—Brother! I stole his key!"

The friar considered. "Methinks it was the Count's key, since it was for his dungeon. But please continue. What did you do then?"

"I left. I climbed back into the wine cellar and heard someone in the passage, so I hastened up the back of the barrel rack so as not to be seen. When the Chief Steward came in, he looked down, not up. He dropped into the dungeon and pulled the hatch shut behind. I climbed off the barrels and put my ear to the wood. Surely enough, there was a click when he shut himself into his cell, and a horrible yell right afterward. 'Thieves! Robbers!' he yelled. Just to be sure he had no more trickery, I rolled a barrel onto the hatch and hastened back to the kitchen."

"With the key?"

"Nay. It's yet on the barrel rack for all I know."

"That explains much, but not completely how the Chief Steward went mad."

Perry drew a deep breath. "To the servants, he was more a

tyrant than any nobleman could ever be. If you upset him, you would be lucky to lose only your position. Even the jailers feared him. He refused their food and water and ordered them never to enter his cell."

"But the Chief Steward said his cell was cleaned daily!"

"Aye, it was, but by the Chief Steward himself. He dared not have his key found by a drudge. Every day he threw the waste from his cell into the pit at the end of the passage. As to food and drink, he commanded the kitchen staff to pass good provisions down the shaft from the kitchen herb garden."

"That is the source of his light?"

Perry shivered. "It *was*. And communication. The garden was not guarded. Once after I was released, I surprised a stranger speaking into the hole. He fled before I could stop him. I have since had the gate locked so the garden can only be entered from the kitchen. But I digress. The day of the feast, the Chief Steward demanded the finest meal I could prepare for the day to follow, or he would see that I would be sent back to the dungeon and never return. I wondered why he chose that day, but now I am sure he ate well enough during the feast while he was up and about the castle. So the next day, I fixed the finest goose I have ever roasted. It was basted with such wonderful spices that the very aroma should make one go mad with hunger. That bird was so warm and plump that the juices fairly poured from it.

"I took his feast into the garden. I called down the hole. 'Here comes your food! Enjoy it!' First I sent down a bottle of the Count's best wine, but somehow I failed to tie a rope to it. It must have smashed, for immediately an angry yell came from below. Then I sent down the goose, but it was such a great goose that it stuck halfway down. I pushed on it with a staff, but that only wedged it tighter. Methinks, though, that the hot juices ran ahead of the fowl so the Chief Steward could smell them, maybe even taste them. I am not certain because the hole was so plugged that I could no longer hear him. Every day since, I have dropped more food and drink down in case the goose has moved, but probably it has not. I do confess, though, that since that day I have not used such good food or wine as the first."

The gray friar became more somber as the cook spoke. His voice grew grayer in the dark. "You say that is your confession?"

"Yea."

"It is not. You have told what happened. To what do you confess?"

Perry hesitated. "I stole a key?"

"Nay, you *moved* a key. To what do you confess?"

There was startled silence. Then, "I—I have driven a man mad!"

"And?"

"And I am starving him!" He tried to control his broken voice. "But the Steward was an evil man!"

"Does a *good* man starve another and drive him mad?"

"NO!" The cook sobbed. "But I hated him!"

The friar leaned back. "Ahh! That is the rest of the confession I had hoped to hear. Now be forgiven by the only One who never had aught to confess."

The miserable man took a deep, shuddering breath. He looked toward his unseen confessor. "But what of penance?"

"Your heart is broken. That will do," answered the friar gently. "But if you will do something good in gratitude for forgiveness, you may feed the wretch in the cell."

The cook was quiet for a minute. "I wish never to return there."

"You can walk in and out. He cannot. Even if he should ever go free, he might never escape the prison he has made for himself. Let us ease his burden if it can be done."

Perry the Poacher set a platter, a chipped dish, and three pewter mugs on a serving tray. He arranged a loaf of bread and a roasted chicken on the platter and set a smaller loaf and half of a chicken on the dish. Then he filled one mug and the pitcher with beer. He set an oil lamp on the tray, took a deep breath, and reluctantly carried the tray from the kitchen to the dark passageway.

Down the stairs he went. There was no sound but his pounding heart as he passed the wine cellar and turned right. Then there were two lights in the passageway: the flickering lamp on his tray and a smoky brand above the jailers' table. The Dungeon Master jumped to his feet and gripped a sword. The headsman surreptitiously slid a white checker off the board.

"Ho! Who goes there?"

"Food for you and the Chief Steward," Perry said. He hoped they would not hear the chatter in his voice.

The Dungeon Master studied the tray and sniffed. "Hmm! Fine fare for a prisoner!"

"Or a madman," added the headsman.

"He is the Chief Steward, prisoner or no. And if the guest merits fine food, so do his hosts." The cook set the platter, pitcher, and two empty tankards on the table, taking care not to disturb the checkers.

"Then long may he be our guest!" the headsman grunted and took half the chicken. The Dungeon Master grabbed the pitcher with one hand and lifted the bar from the dungeon door with the other. Only a little beer sloshed out. He pulled the protesting door open and waited for the cook.

Perry hesitated, finally passed through, and reluctantly descended. The smells and dripping noises had not changed since the time of his residence. Neither had the squeaking rats, nor the slippery floors. The only difference was invisible. The black hatch in the ceiling looked the same as before but now, he knew, was weighted shut by four hundred pounds of wine.

The Dungeon Master unlocked the cell. He took a deep swallow from the pitcher and hurried back up the stairs before his partner could finish off the food. Perry was left alone to face the man he had driven insane. He pulled the door open.

Lamplight reflected from shards of glass and from a pair of wild eyes. The Chief Steward sat on the floor directly below the shaft to the surface, with his knees drawn to his chest and his arms tightly wrapped around his legs. He rocked forward and backward while flies commuted between the shaft and his filthy body. His clothing was stained with blood from glass cuts. His lips were cracked. Perry could see where the Steward had licked moisture from the cell walls. The Poacher had done the same when food and water were slow in coming.

"I have food and drink," he offered.

No answer. The prisoner continued to rock.

"Bread. Drink. Meat."

"NO! No goose!" croaked the Steward. He scuttled away from Perry and cowered in the furthest corner of the cell.

"Not goose. Chicken." Perry tore off a leg and crept forward with the food extended in front of him. The prisoner hugged himself more tightly and began to moan.

Perry drew back his arm. Setting the chicken leg back on the plate, he took the loaf of bread and broke off an end. He dipped it into the beer and offered it as he had the chicken. "Thirsty?" He squatted and duck-walked toward the Steward until the sodden morsel contacted the miserable man's lips.

The Steward tentatively stuck his swollen tongue between his lips and tested the bread. He sucked the beer from it as if from a sponge. Suddenly he clawed the bread away from Perry and buried his face in it.

The startled cook jumped back. He slid the plate and mug toward the prisoner. "I will leave these. Eat."

He left the cell and began to push the door shut. A cry stopped him.

The prisoner sprang to his pallet and pawed beneath it, searching for something. He started to scream. "Dark! No, not dark!"

Perry grabbed the lamp and ran to the stairs. He pounded on the door at the top. Eventually it opened, revealing a mellow Dungeon Master with beer on his breath and chicken grease on his whiskers. The cook sprang through the door, and the jailer closed it behind him.

"But the Steward's cell is yet open!" gasped Perry.

"So?" asked the Dungeon Master. "This door is closed. There are no other prisoners. He has nowhere to go."

Perry thought of the hatch to the wine cellar but remembered it was blocked. "So be it." He left with his heart still pounding.

The next day, Perry took another meal like the first to the Chief Steward. He also dragged behind him a broom and a gunnysack. The jailers curiously eyed the assortment but did not ask questions lest their food get cold.

"You need not accompany me," the cook told them, "as the cell is already unlocked."

The Dungeon Master shrugged and let him in.

Perry set the broom and bag inside the dungeon door. He cautiously descended with the lamp and food, wondering where the steward might be, but nobody was in the passage. He pulled open the cell door, and the steward was crouched below the dark shaft as he had been the day before. The plate and mug sat empty on the floor. Not a chicken bone was to be seen.

"I have more food." He swapped full dishes for empty ones

and stepped back.

The steward crept toward them, keeping his eyes on the cook. Then he grabbed the food and ate noisily. He downed the beer. He belched. He smiled.

Perry edged toward the door.

"No! Not dark!" screamed the Chief Steward.

Perry left the lamp on the floor, just outside the open cell door. The flame was almost bright in the blackness of the dungeon. Perry followed his own wavering shadow back to the stair and returned with the broom and bag. The prisoner had crawled toward the lamp and was staring intently into the flame. The cook circled past him and shoved his broom handle into the ceiling shaft. Flies swarmed downward as the broom poked upward. Suddenly an avalanche of rotting meat and falling bottles cascaded into the room. They were immediately followed by a brilliant flood of bluish light. The startled prisoner squinted and rubbed his eyes. Squealing with glee, he ran into the sunbeam and stared upward.

The cook began to sweep. He piled goose fragments, bottle shards, and uneaten meals into the bag while the Chief Steward gibbered happily. The cook set the broom in a corner and dragged the bag with one hand while carrying the tray and lamp in the other. The bag bumped up the steps behind him. The Steward was still jabbering when the headsman opened the door.

Perry returned the next day. The jailers were pleased to see him. "We gave our guest a lamp," reported the Dungeon Master. "Now he does not scream. And we opened the rest of the cells as well. Nobody else is home."

Indeed, when Perry reached the bottom of the stairs, a light wavered in the passage. He stiffened. But it was only the Chief Steward singing nonsense and sweeping the entire dungeon. The Steward spotted him and ran happily back to his cell, where he squatted and waited to be served. This became the daily routine.

There was only one problem with the Chief Steward's custodial improvements. As the dungeon became cleaner, the Steward himself became even more noticeable. The man was a walking cesspool. His clothing, unchanged since he had lost his key, had accumulated much of the filth he swept up.

Finally the cook had had enough. One day while he was stirring a great pot of soup in the kitchen, he came to a decision. "Stir this, and mind it does not stick," he ordered a kitchen drudge and pivoted to leave.

"But, sir, you have the..."

"No, *you* have the duty!" Perry cut him off and exited the kitchen. He went straight to the servants' wing of the castle. Looking around to be sure he was not seen, he stole to the end of the hall and furtively opened the door to the Chief Steward's quarters. He entered and quietly shut it behind him. The Chief Steward must have had the only door in the castle that did not squeak, and probably not by accident. The room was as it had been left. A layer of dust covered everything.

Almost everything. A trail of footprints led through the dust from the doorway to an inner chamber. Perry scanned for a weapon and saw none until he looked in his own hand. There was the ladle. He momentarily wondered what the drudge might use to stir the soup, but then returned to the matter at hand. Raising the ladle like a cudgel, he tiptoed to the second doorway. There was a little noise to the left of the door, just out of sight. Perry waited. He was not brave enough to attack an unknown assailant.

Somebody backed into his field of view. Somebody female. She did not seem to have noticed him. Perry inched forward. The surly maid was bent over a drawer she had just opened.

"What are...?"

The maid yelped but did not turn around. She gripped the sides of the drawer and leaned heavily on her arms while she caught her breath. "So I am dead. Just kill me quickly." Her usual surly demeanor had not departed.

Perry lowered his ladle. "For what? Stealing? I've not yet seen you steal. Prying? Usually not a capital offense. Being where you do not belong? Then I am dead too."

She faced him. "Then why are you here? To steal, or to pry?"

"Neither. I am here for clothing. But I might ask you the same question."

She nearly smiled. "To pry. But see what I have found. It *is* worth stealing!" She pointed into the drawer. It was littered with jewelry and gold coins.

The cook shook his head. "It is not. With it you would buy a dungeon and hire a headsman for yourself. But what is this?" He reached into the back of the drawer and drew out a heavily jeweled ring. "This is too fine a bauble for a Chief Steward. What else might there be?" He tugged the next drawer open. Inside rested a pair of silver candlesticks, an intricate crucifix nearly two feet high, several fine knives, and a golden serving platter.

He inspected the platter. "Methinks its mate lives in the sideboard and only comes out for feasts." He looked at the surly maid. "Mark what I said. This thief bought the dungeon and lost his head even before his theft was discovered."

"Then we should leave before anyone knows we were here!" She started for the door.

He caught her arm and pointed at their footprints. "Somebody *would* notice, and we would be dead. Truth comes out whenever it chooses. We must report ourselves before someone else does."

"*What?*" The surly maid returned to form. "You mean to report me and spare yourself!"

"If I were to call you a thief, you would do the same to me. The Count would not know whom to believe, and we might both be finished. Instead we will both call the thief a thief. I came for clothing for the prisoner. You came to clean. We found stolen goods and reported the thief, who is already known to be a knave." He scooped up the ring and the platter. "Let us show this much to the Count." Then remembering why he had come in the first place, he gathered a set of the Chief Steward's clothes.

Ten minutes later, Count Otto examined the platter and the ring. "The ring looks familiar, but it is not mine. The Chief Steward must have stolen it before he came to us here. But the platter I know. It is worth more than his head."

"Begging your pardon, my lord," began Perry, "but he is worse than dead already. With some care, though, he might regain his mind and we could learn whom he served. If he gets his head back, then you can take it from him."

The Count eyed the cook. "I have heard of your care for the prisoner. The jailers are looking fat and happy, too. My meals have been good, even if we are going through more chickens than usual. We have not lost a chamberlain to the axe for several weeks now, and my barber no longer trembles when he shaves me. That is very good, my throat thinks. The rest of the servants are more agreeable than they have been in a year. Even the surly maid is only grumpy these days."

She scowled.

"I seem not to need the Chief Steward to run the castle. He seems not to need his rooms. You may take them as your quarters. Then you will not have to creep in for fresh clothing for the prisoner, and"—the Count turned to the surly maid—-

"you will not have to creep in to clean."

A few minutes later, Perry the Poacher entered the kitchen with a bundle of clean clothes and fresh rags. He observed that the drudge was stirring the pot with a broom, and made a mental note to eat leftovers that evening. Then he fixed up the usual tray of chicken, bread, and beer, but not soup, for the diners in the dungeon, and laid it atop a nearly full pail of water. He carried the bundle in his left hand, grasped the pail handle with his right, and started toward the back hall. It would be a slow trip.

"Give me the pail." The surly maid had come up behind him. "I know where you are bound."

He stopped. "You would go there?"

"No. I will take the pail as far as the corner past the wine cellar, but no further. If you should try to carry all of this, you would break your neck on the first stair. Then I would have to scrub you *and* the food off the steps."

Perry smiled a bit. "Then for your sake you may carry the pail." He set it down. "But you will need a light."

"I have one."

They proceeded down the stairs in silence. No sooner had they reached the bottom than she asked him, "Why do you do this?"

Perry thought for a moment. "I don't know. Gratitude, I think."

She stared, unbelieving. "To *him?* You must be mad!" She turned back toward the stairs. The pail sloshed. The flame of her lamp drew a flickering arc when she whirled, following the wick like the tail of a comet.

Perry's lamp did not move. "Nay, but that I am *not* he. I am delivered."

Her lamp hesitated. The flame again rose straight. "That is worth something, I suppose." The glow completed another semicircle, but more slowly, and proceeded down the hall in silence.

They reached the corner past the wine cellar, and the surly maid set down the pail and her light. She leaned around the corner. Not twenty feet away, the headsman and Dungeon Master were engrossed in their game of checkers. Neither one noticed her. A heavily scored chopping block about two feet high stood near the wall. On it lay an axe, black except for the edges of two curved blades, each about twice as wide as a neck. The point of a sword was embedded in the side of the block, with the handle within easy reach of the seated Dungeon Master. A pike lay along the opposite side of the hall, and a coiled whip hung from a peg wedged between stones in the wall.

The jailers' lantern flickered yellow and orange, gasping for good air and generating a cloud of smoke that embraced the sooty ceiling. The flame dimly reflected off the sharpened edges of the axe, sword, and pike but made no dent on the blackness in the doorway behind the men. The Chief Steward's loud, tuneless song poured through the open door.

The maid quickly turned, picked up her light, and hurried back to the world above.

Perry watched her go. Returning to the task at hand, he tossed the bundle of clothes around the corner. The jailers still paid no attention. He set his tray back onto the pail to carry them in one hand and the lamp in the other. The smell of food accomplished what noise and lanterns had not. The Dungeon Master slid a pile of captured checkers to the side and motioned for the tray to be set there. The headsman looked into the pail, then at Perry.

"No soup?"

"It was poorly seasoned."

"Then I shall soften my bread in beer instead." The headsman jumped a king and reached for the loaf.

The Dungeon Master grabbed the pitcher. "For two kings

you may."

The headsman's eyes flashed in the lamplight. "As you wish." He jumped the last pair of the Dungeon Master's kings. "I win."

The Dungeon Master did not take it well, so Perry let himself through the door. Leaving the food and lamp at the top of the stair, he gingerly descended with the pail and the bag of clothes. He set the pail on the bottom step and the bundle next to it. His nose told him that the Steward was nearby. Perry dropped one rag into the pail and laid a folded one on the floor beside it. Then he retrieved the lamp. The Steward ran out of the cell across from his own, where he had been cleaning. He smiled broadly and started to jabber, but then he noticed that his benefactor bore no meal.

"Eat?" Wide eyes stared questioningly from a smudged face.

"Yes, but first, wash."

The prisoner's mouth hung open. "Wha?"

"Yes. Wash. You are filthy." Perry pointed to the bucket.

The Steward looked at himself. He raised an arm a bit and sniffed. His nose wrinkled. He picked at his sleeve.

"Take them off. You have made the dungeon nicer. Now make yourself nicer."

"Make Papa happy?" The prisoner's eyes reflected hope.

Perry jolted. "I'm not your papa!"

"Make Papa happy?" The eyes pleaded.

He sighed. "Yes, yes, it'll make Papa happy."

The Steward grinned. He ran to the end of the passage and tore off his clothes. He flung them into the waste pit and ran back naked. Perry retreated up the stairs. The Steward grabbed the soggy rag from the pail and began to wash. He worked as thoroughly upon himself as he had the dungeon. Finally he poured the pail over his head and patted himself dry with the other rag.

"Make Papa happy now?"

"Papa will be happier when you are dressed."

The Steward donned fresh clothes as rapidly as he could. His hair was matted and stringy, and his face was in that uncertain stage between a bad shave and a bad beard, but he was clean.

"Make Papa happy now?"

"Papa is happy."

The Chief Steward squealed and clapped. "Now eat?"

Perry brought the food and drink from the top of the stairs. It was the first time in a week he could do it without cringing. "Eat."

Bathing became a weekly ritual. Perry knew that excessive bathing was dangerous, but the Steward was an exceptional case.

"May the Chief Steward drown in his bucket!" muttered the surly maid to herself as she reentered the lighted world after the second week. As time passed, she spent less time muttering about the Steward and more time contemplating Perry. "An odd man, that," she muttered several weeks later.

One day the cook emerged from the kitchen with his tray for the dungeon just as Friar Fred happened by for an apple. The friar nodded at him. Perry set down the tray.

"Friar Fred, I do not understand the Chief Steward."

"God alone understands him."

"Why does he call me Papa? After what I did—"

The friar raised his hand. "Stop! You are forgiven. Do not forget that. But as to the Steward, he does not know what you did. He only knows that you brought him light, and you care for him."

The Poacher stopped and thought. "Indeed, that may be. But he grows stranger and stranger. Until recently he spent all his time cleaning the dungeon, but of late he has done nothing but scribble on the walls."

The friar's eyes widened. "Oh? And what does he scribble?"

"I have no way of knowing. And I doubt the Chief Steward can read."

"I would be interested to see if he writes or only scribbles."

"That is what I hoped you would say. Shall we find out?"

The men proceeded toward the dungeon. The jailers grunted and pointed to the unbarred door behind them. The headsman took a chicken wing, and the Dungeon Master took the headsman's checker. A discussion ensued. Poacher and preacher, forgotten for the moment, descended the steep steps.

It was quiet in the dungeon except for a scratching noise inside one cell. The visitors looked in. A lamp rested on the floor. The Chief Steward was intently marking on a sooty wall with a rusty nail, oblivious to all else. His shadow obscured the place where he was working. Two other walls were completely covered with inscriptions.

Perry set down the dish and mug. "I have a guest."

The Steward turned around. Seeing the priest, he smiled and began to gabble. He took Friar Fred by the arm and led him to the corner nearest the door. He pointed to the upper left corner and grinned expectantly.

"Call me Ishmael," read the friar.

The Chief Steward squealed and clapped. Then he grabbed a loaf of bread from the dish. Stuffing as much as would fit into his mouth, he raced back with the rest of the loaf to where he had left off and resumed scratching. He would scribble with his right hand and stuff his mouth with the left. He paid no more attention to his visitors.

Friar Fred moved back into the passageway. Perry followed. "What do you make of it?"

The friar shook his head. "It is indeed writing, but there is no sense in it. It says nothing of the Ishmael I know about. But what is this?"

They were about to pass through one of the many low arches that separated the cells. Neatly scratched into the keystone overhead was, *Jeremiah was a bullfrog.*

"Foolishness or blasphemy, I cannot tell," observed the friar.

"There is much more." Perry opened the next cell and raised his torch.

"*'Twas the best of times; 'twas the worst of times,*" Friar Fred read, then faced his companion. "This also is beyond understanding." Curious, he entered the next cell.

"*E=MC².*" The friar crossed himself. "Alas, this is perhaps worse than gibberish! The walls are covered with arcana that are not even words." They quickly left for another chamber.

"*It was a dark and stormy night.* We are back to words, but the writing is wretched."

Back in the passage, the next arch said, *She wore an itsy bitsy, teeny weeny, yellow polka dot beak eeny.*

"Lewd, I suspect. But perhaps not. I know not what an eeny is." The friar escaped into the nearest cell.

"*High in an arched castle window, a gossamer lacework of spiders' silk shimmered in the morning sun,*" he read. "The worst of all! I can take no more." He dusted off his hands and headed for the stairs, not even reading inscriptions as they passed beneath them.

Perry walked beside him. "A pity, I had hoped..."

Friar Fred smiled gently in the dark. "You had hoped that something good would come of the Steward. Something has, but not in him."

"YEEEEE-HAWW!"

Count Otto sat bolt upright in bed. His heart pounded so loudly that the sound seemed to come from outdoors. No, there *was* pounding outdoors, as well as inside his body. He leapt out of bed and ran to the window. Somebody was beating at the town gate. Knights who should have been patrolling the walls were instead running out of the guardroom and dragging their armor behind them.

The watchman was running to and fro, crying, "My bugle! Who's got my bugle?"

"You lost it at darts, remember?" yelled the Captain of the Guard.

"But I need it!"

"Forget the bugle! Just sound the alarm any way you can!"

"HELP! HELLLLP!" The watchman ran to and fro in the dark.

There was barely enough daylight yet to wake a rooster, but the sky glowed yellow just outside the wall. Torches illuminated the bridge and the road behind it.

"PAR-TY! PAR-TY! PAR-TY!" yelled the mob. Flames moved up and down with the chant.

"SHUT YALL'S YAPS!" commanded a voice in front. "THEY MIGHT BE SLEEPIN' YET!"

Otto knew that voice! Surely he wouldn't be attacked by his old friend….

"HEY, OTTO! IT'S ME, ROLLO! WHYN'CHA LET US IN? SOME OF US GOTTA USE THE BATHROOM!"

"Hurry!" pleaded a voice from the mob.

Count Otto leaned out the window. Cobwebs stuck to his

face. "Let them in," he called to the gatekeeper stumbling up the road.

"My lord, I'm not on duty for another hour!"

Otto sighed. "So be it. Your first duty when you *are* on duty will be to clean the bridge!" The gatekeeper hesitated only a second before running to his post.

The gate creaked open. In came a jostling mob with Count Rollo at the head. They were definitely his knights. Only Rollo's forces sported helmets with wide brims all the way around and a crease across the top from front to back. They jostled to be at the head of the line for the necessary room.

Inside the castle, Otto's new chamberlain was trying to get his lord dressed. The chamberlain himself was only half dressed, but duty came first. It was difficult because his lord would not stand still. The Count turned from the window and hurried to the doorway. The chamberlain pivoted and followed, buttoning and tying as he went. "Get chamberpots!" called Otto into the hall.

The bedraggled surly maid complied, surlier than ever. She dragged a clanking bag out the front door of the castle, knowing full well who would have to clean them afterward.

"I'll assign you a drudge," offered Perry as he raced past her to the kitchen. "A surly one," he said quietly after safely out of earshot.

Otto was a short distance behind the maid. The chamberlain was right behind Otto. The barber brought up the rear, yawning and whipping up froth in a shaving basin. Rollo came around the corner from the necessary room, looking considerably more comfortable than the mob pressing the other way. One advantage of nobility is the divine right to cut into line. He tipped his hat to Otto.

"What is the meaning of this?" Otto demanded. The barber smeared suds on his face. The maid began flinging chamberpots into the crowd. Knights scrambled for them like children for

89

prizes at a party. The air was full of men's voices, metallic squeaks, and flying pots.

"We're here for the picnic."

Otto jumped and nearly got his throat cut. *"What* picnic?"

Rollo smiled slyly. "The one y'all fergot to tell us about."

"There *is* no picnic!" Shaving suds splattered upon the explosion of *picnic.*

"Well, be that way then." Rollo wiped specks of foam off his tunic. "Me, yer best friend, and you won't invite us. At least I thought we wuz friends." He beckoned his knights. "Hey, fellers!"

This could get ugly. "Never mind, Rollo, we'll have a picnic. And you all are invited."

"YAYYYY!" The knights cheered, then looked around with embarrassment and shushed each other.

"But Rollo, where did you hear about a picnic?" mumbled Otto through a towel. The shave was complete. The barber eyed the stubble on Count Rollo's face and looked questioningly at Otto. Otto shook his head.

"From the white knights," answered Rollo.

"White knights?"

"Sure." He leaned against a balustrade. "Me an' the boys here was plinkin' rabbits with bows and arrows when a line o' knights come over the ridge. White ones. So's I trotted up to the boss an' asked where they wuz goin, seein' as how they wuzn't my knights but wuz ridin' through my county."

Rollo scratched his side. "I could tell the boss didn't want to let on, but I kinda kept after him. He finally got fed up an' said, 'To a picnic.' 'A picnic?' sez I. 'Sounds like fun! Where?' He sorta clammed up, but I kept on him. My boys heard, though. They like picnics an' started comin' round us. 'Finally he sighed real hard an' rolled his eyes an' said, 'Okay, then, over t' Otto's place.' He said it different, of course, but you git the idea." Rollo's hurt look returned. "Now I know why he didn't let on. Y'all didn't want us to come."

"But I—we—know of no picnic!"

His friend's eyes brightened. "Oh, I git it! It was gonna be a surprise!" His face fell. "But I done ruined it. Sorry, ol' pal."

Otto was not comforted by the thought of a surprise. "No, I'm glad you ruined their surprise. They may be up to no good."

"Now don't get all riled up," Rollo corrected. "They wuz wearin' white outfits. An' they didn't have no masks neither."

Obviously Count Rollo would not be dissuaded. "Well, then, we will surprise them instead. They are not expecting you. And I will invite my own knights as well." Otto turned to his barber. "Summon my heralds." The barber hurried off, razor and basin in hand. There could not be much time if Rollo and his men had already arrived. "I don't see the white knights yet."

Rollo grinned. "Naw, they wuz in too much of a hurry. So we beat 'em here."

"What do you mean?"

"Well, we said we'd like to go along just as soon as we rustled up a couple chickens an' changed clothes, but their ol' boss wouldn't wait. So off they went. We hustled back to the castle an' got ready an' took the shortcut."

"Shortcut?"

"It's a secret!" he whispered hoarsely. Then he considered. "'Course if it's a secret, y'all wouldn't know about it. Anyways, we took it."

"When did all this happen?"

"Yesterday mornin'." He closed his eyes.

"That must be some shortcut." Rollo's county was normally a three-day trip on bad roads. If the white knights rode hard, they might arrive late the next afternoon. "Did you travel all night?"

"Yep." Rollo yawned.

Sleeping soldiers would not be much help. "Well, Rollo, the picnic won't be until tomorrow afternoon. Perhaps you and your men would wish to rest before then. Meanwhile we will make ready to surprise the white knights."

"Thanks. Don't mind if we do. NAPTIME!" he yelled. Knights dropped wherever they stood. Count Rollo flopped onto a bench. Count Otto headed toward the castle door.

"Otto?"

"Yes?"

"Is it y'all's birthday?"

"No."

"Good, cuz I didn't bring no present." Rollo began to snore.

Heralds were arriving. They were not too awake, and a few tripped over knights.

"Quickly, summon the barons!" Otto ordered. "Tell them to prepare for battle!" Then remembering Rollo's forces, he added, "And a picnic."

The heralds stared at the Count and at each other.

"Go!"

They went, shaking their heads.

Picnic or not, the men would have to eat. Otto summoned Perry. "Prepare to feed an army for two days at least. Pack provisions into picnic baskets. Rustle up a Maypole to keep Rollo's men happy."

"But it isn't May, my lord."

"So find a June pole or July pole or whatever other pole you need!"

"It's September, my lord."

"A September pole, then!"

Perry collared the surly drudge who had just finished cleaning chamberpots and set him to work on plates in the scullery. He assigned the surly maid to locate a September pole, which only made her surlier. Then he betook himself to the kitchen.

Baron Bertram and twenty knights arrived just before noon with wicker baskets hanging from their lances. An hour later, Baron Baxter's thirty men rode in with chickens spitted on theirs. Baron Aaron marched at the head of three dozen soldiers with broadswords and apples. Baroness Beatrice (Benjamin was off on a Crusade) brought picnic blankets and fifteen bowmen. Baron Barrie's thirty-eight men were armed with maces and croquet mallets. Baron Bud's twenty-four soldiers lugged eighteen battleaxes and six kegs. Bartholomew the Baron's soldiers had recently succumbed to a bad case of Vikings, so he was accompanied by a hundred serfs with buckets full of wildflowers. Baron Bernie did not arrive. No herald dared across the bridge with his invitation.

The little room by the castle gate was opened. Bags of stones were hoisted into a room directly above the gate, so they could be dropped through the murder hole in the floor onto unwelcome visitors. Servants hauled barrels of oil to the top of the wall, where they emptied them into a large cauldron suspended from an iron tripod. Smoke wafted from a fire already burning beneath it. The white knights were not likely to arrive for another day, but it would be wise to preheat the oil just in case. And as long as it was ready, Perry tossed in a few chickens. Grease splattered.

"Mmm! Somethin' smells good!" Count Rollo smacked his lips and opened his eyes about two in the afternoon. In the square he beheld a tall pole festooned with long ribbons in autumn colors. "Hey! Git up!" he yelled to his sleeping men. "They're doin' all the work!" Two yawning warriors wandered toward the September pole, but a stern word from Rollo brought them back. "Not till tomorrow! You boys help git ready for the picnic."

It was a busy afternoon. Sparks flew where Otto's men sharpened swords and axes. Rollo's men erected trestle tables in the town square. Otto's archers strung their bows. Rollo's men set up horseshoe pits. Drudges filled fire buckets with water. Rollo's men decorated tables with discarded wildflowers. The gatekeeper tested the portcullis. Rollo's men commandeered bags for sack races. Serfs mowed tall grass and weeds near the moat so attackers would not be concealed. Rollo's men, noting the readiness of other knights' weapons, sharpened and oiled their own so they too would be ready for contests.

Shadows were getting long by the time preparations were complete. Knights opened picnic baskets and began to chew. Servants threw fried chickens from the top of the wall. A few of the birds were missing a bite or two before launch. A few of the servants had chicken on their breath. Counts Otto and Rollo surveyed the scene from the castle tower, drumsticks in hand. "Ain't the surprise picnic supposed to be tomorrow?" Rollo asked between bites.

Otto swallowed from his mug. "Aye, but this food is here today. 'Twould be a shame to let it spoil. We will see what our guests bring tomorrow."

"Why not? It's their surprise."

Rollo's eyes scanned the town. He was having trouble waiting for the picnic. So were his men, who gazed longingly at the September pole.

Otto looked over the countryside, wondering where the morrow's visitors would first appear. Would they take the road? It was the fastest way, but the most obvious.

Might they attack from Yonder Wood? No, it had a dragon.

The swamp? Quicksand and mosquitoes guarded that route.

How about the river? Probably not. Armored knights were not fond of tippy boats.

"Well, lookit that!" exclaimed Rollo around a bite of chicken.

"What?"

Rollo had focused his attention on the river. "Reckon it must be the woodcutters." A collection of dots was floating around the uppermost bend, two miles from the castle.

Otto's mouth went dry. He raced to the opposite window and leaned out. Below him on the wall, the watchman watched a girl serving boiled turnips from a metal tub.

"WA—WA—WA—" yelled Otto, but the watchman wasn't listening. Otto took another pull of ale to lubricate his voice, but only a tablespoon was left. He flung the empty mug out the window. The ensuing crash got the watchman's attention, and he looked around to see where it had come from. Otto threw a chicken carcass at him. The watchman looked up.

"Oh! Sorry, my lord!" The watchman took a breath. "NINE O'CLOCK AND—" A fish head caught him on the cheek.

"SOUND THE ALARM!" Otto yelled. The startled watchman reached for his bugle, but he had not won it back. Instead he yanked the serving girl's tub from her hands and dumped the turnips into the crowd below. That was not wholly effective either, so he beat on the tub with a hambone. All eyes turned his direction. Realizing he did not know what the peril was, he employed a general alarm.

"HELP! HELLLLP!" The watchman ran back and forth, pointing toward the Count. The Count pointed toward the river. Knights dropped their picnic baskets, grabbed their weapons, and ran to the walls. The serving girl rescued her tub and leveled the watchman with it.

"Serves him right!" growled Otto.

A flotilla of boats was coming downstream. Above the clatter of oars could be heard sailors singing rude songs. They dropped anchor only a furlong away where the river ran nearest to the castle. Otto's knights peered nervously from the battlements. Rollo stood perplexed. "Why's everybody so jumpy? We're all ready for the picnic. Them ain't the white knights anyway, just a buncha woodcutters."

A roar arose from the boats when a scow rounded the bend and dropped anchor in their midst. Mounted on it amidships was a wooden frame with a spoked capstan protruding from the side. A timber boom reached toward the sky. Flying from the boom was a black flag:

Count Rollo gaped with disbelief. "Them stinkin' pirates stole the rattrap!"

Otto looked at him. "Do you know something of this?"

"Sure. The woodcutters made it. I bet them pirates killed all of the elves too!" A tear started down his cheek.

There was no time to continue the conversation. A pitch pipe sounded from the scow. Four men hummed in harmony, then began to sing and wind the capstan.

> *"A river pyrate's life for me;*
> *I've had enough of the open sea.*
> *Now if perchance my shyppe should synke,*
> *Mine hedde may stay above the drynke!"*

The boom started to bend away from the castle. The scow

began to tilt.

> "Yo ho, avast, and blow the man downe;
> I'm coming tomorrow to plunder your towne—"

The scow suddenly tipped. The boom arched downward onto a canoe carrying three pirates. Only one pirate was in the way. The other two dove into the river, and a V-shaped wake sped their direction.

The scow, though listing dangerously, did not quite capsize. As many pirates as would fit leaned off the rail on the high side while the business end of the weapon lay athwart the canoe. The singers resumed their business, and the scow slowly righted itself.

> "A trusty compass need I nott,
> Nor rolls of ocean maps to plott.
> No Northe or Southe or Easte or Weste:
> Uppstreme or downe; forget all the reste!
>
> And when the wicked storm do howle,
> I pop ashore and steal a towle.
> So Davy Jones, don't wait for me—
> I'm anchored fast beneath a tree.
>
> 'Tis bounty always close at hand;
> We're never, ever far from land
> Wyth golde and grogge and agreeable maides,
> And piles of jewels in various grades.
>
> And tho I may look back at tymes
> On lands of kumquats, fygges, and lymes,
> I eat roaste beefe whene'er I wyshe;
> Because I've had me fylle of fysshe!"

The winding and the song were complete. Thanks to pirates still leaning on the scow rail opposite, the boom had risen enough so the cracked canoe could escape to the waterfall. A rowboat detached from the flotilla, belching black smoke. Pirates maneuvered their craft beneath the end of the boom. Straining, they manhandled a rock about two feet in diameter into the leather sling. The pouch sagged to the bottom of the boat but did not break. Then the sailors reached down and gingerly hoisted two planks, atop which rested half a barrel of flaming tar. Several false moves later, they finally managed to balance the barrel on top of the rock. Their boat lay pinned beneath the load. They would have an excellent view of the launch.

Black smoke billowed into the reddening sky. "FIRE!" yelled the pirate king. A sailor on the scow knocked the capstan catch free with a mallet, and the boom shot upward.

But only a little way. The pirates were better at music than they were at physics. The ammunition was too heavy. The scow flipped sideways and slipped halfway below the surface of the water, but not before pirates along the rail were launched in short screaming arcs toward the far bank. The bank was out of range. V-shaped wakes sped toward the splashdown zone. Greenie caught one pirate in midflight. His tail wagged.

The weapon was not a total failure. The rock rose twenty feet, changed its mind, and plummeted through the bottom of the rowboat. The flaming, tumbling tar barrel sailed upward like a meteor with no sense of direction. A pinwheel of black and orange streamers erupted, fell, and splattered. Yelling pirates raced their craft downstream ahead of flames afloat on the water. Shortly only a crackling scow and a burning boom were left. Large heads and spade-shaped tails were silhouetted against the flames and the setting sun. V-shaped wakes crisscrossed and shimmered in darkening shades of red and yellow.

Perry the Poacher had brought a plate of cold salmon to the spectators in the tower. He stood behind the two Counts, intently studying the scene past their shoulders.

Count Rollo slapped Otto on the back. "Well, at least y'all don't have no pirates no more. Serves 'em right fer killin' them elves!"

Otto shook his head. "No, the survivors will gather downstream at the bridge."

"Not after tonight, my lord." Perry continued to gaze out the window.

The Count looked at his cook. "What do you mean?"

"I have made plans. The pirates should be gone before noon."

"I would have to see it to believe it!"

"You would have to be there by dawn then. I must prepare before light."

Otto was intrigued. "Very well. Tell the chamberlain to wake me an hour before the rooster would. I shall sleep clothed, and we will ride together." He turned to Rollo. "Do you want to come?"

"No way! I'm goin' to bed. Gotta be at my best for the picnic." He padded down the steep stairway.

Otto grunted and followed.

Perry took a last look at the glowing wreckage, picked up his tray, and brought up the rear.

The knock on the door came entirely too soon. Otto momentarily wondered why he was still dressed. Then he remembered. His decision to go larking with Perry the Poacher

99

did not seem nearly as good as it had a few hours earlier, but it was too late to change his mind. People already knew he was going. The chamberlain, carrying a flickering lamp, led the Count down dark stairs to the main hall where Perry waited with a large bag. The chamberlain left them the lamp and stumbled back to the servants' quarters. A yawning door warden opened the front entrance. Still yawning, he shut the castle up behind them while they dragged the bag to the town gate.

The bag was not heavy, just bulky. The main gate would not open for another two hours. A bleary-eyed gatekeeper unbarred the postern gate. This small, zigzag tunnel was constructed just wide enough for a man to pass sideways through the wall, and it opened onto the plank ledge that the plumber had used. Timbers supporting the ledge could be pulled into the wall to drop the plank into the moat.

"Mind the trip rope," warned the gatekeeper.

Otto nodded.

Halfway through the zigzag passage, a rope stretched across just above floor level. One end of the rope was tied to a ring fixed in the stones. On the opposite side of the passage, the rope was tied to a pole that propped a wooden board against an eight-inch square opening in the ceiling. A large cavity above the board was full of loose sand. It opened at the top into the same little room that housed the lever for the moat. Anyone who stumbled over the rope would dislodge the board. Gatekeepers hated cleaning up after such events. (There had once been a second postern gate at the back of the town, but it had been jammed shut for forty years by two tons of sand and a clumsy thief.) Another rope lay on the bottom of the passage and extended below the door, so a person could safely dislodge the pole and block the tunnel from the town side.

The cook preceded his lord into the passage. The bag rode between them. It took some doing to force it around the first corner in the passage. After that was accomplished, Otto hoisted the bag over the trip rope and Perry pulled it toward himself. It caught on the post. Nobody breathed. Otto pushed his arms between the wall and the bag, prying the fabric away from the pole. Perry pulled at the sack from the opposite side, and it began to move. The pole stayed put. Both men exhaled.

Then there was one more corner. Otto felt the trip rope against his ankle as he shoved the bag toward Perry. Finally the sack began to slide toward the exit. Perry stepped out onto the ledge and sidestepped toward the bridge. The bag extruded from the portal. He slid it toward himself, leaving room for the Count to follow. Backs against the wall, men and bag gingerly slid sideways onto the bridge. Never before had it felt so wide.

The gatekeeper listened from the opposite side of the wall. As soon as it was clear that they had safely traversed the passage, he bolted the postern gate shut and returned to his cot.

They waited a minute while their hearts slowed down. "You would have done this yourself?" Otto asked.

"I would have tried, my lord."

Two large black horses were hobbled beneath the archway just outside the closed main gate. "This is not my horse," observed Otto.

"Nor is it thy saddle. These are draft animals."

Perry removed the hobbles. They clop-clop-clopped across the drawbridge and down the dark road. An owl hooted ahead of them.

"Can anybody creep in and out of town this way?" Otto whispered.

"Nay, my lord," whispered Perry. "I have been planning since I heard of the pirates at the bridge. Your men trust me."

It was a dark night. Starlight barely lit stubbly fields and the road. Then came Pigtruffle Thicket and the hills beyond, where woods on either side blocked all light except occasional patches of sky directly overhead. A little farther along after their eyes had adjusted somewhat, they could discern a weedy clearing that had once lain between the crossroad and an inn. Only wild animals lodged there anymore. Perry glanced at the ruined building, then turned onto the leftward track. They were plunged into darkness. Trees arched over the path. A rustle and the scream of a rabbit could be heard from the bracken beside them. Some fox would eat well that morning. Both men jumped at the noise. Then it was back to buzzing mosquitoes and the monotonous splash of hooves in puddles.

They rounded a bend shortly afterward. Fifty yards ahead, a dark line bisected a faint ribbon of reflected starlight. A distant rumble from the waterfall accompanied soprano mosquitoes, alto splish-splashes beneath their feet, and baritone toads.

Perry halted. "It is good we have a new moon tonight," he whispered. He led the horses off the road and hitched them to a wagon hidden in the brush. Perched atop the wagon was a large wooden chest.

Perry opened his sack. Each horse was issued a nose bag filled with grain so there would be no whinnying. Next he pulled out piles of rags. One by one, he shod the horses' feet with cloth. Then he laid rags ahead of the wagon's wheels and led the horses three feet forward. The axles squeaked. Perry reached deeper into his bag and drew out a jug of something.

"Chicken fat," he murmured, and liberally poured it onto all four axle sleeves. Next he tied rags around the circumferences of the wooden wheels. Finally he led the horses back onto the road. The squealing axles became silent within a few feet.

"Wait here, if you please," whispered Perry. Otto could dimly see the outline of his cook leading the wagon onto the bridge. The horses pulled like the cart was heavy. Their muffled hooves and the wagon's wheels could not be heard over the din of mosquitoes, frogs, and the distant waterfall. Otto slapped at buzzing assailants. His drowsy mind wandered down philosophical paths. Mosquitoes ate Counts. Toads ate mosquitoes. It was a humbling thought.

A sudden noise by his ear snatched him back from philosophy. It sounded like a horse sneezing into a nose bag. It felt like it too. Flying oats, not too dry, peppered his cheek. Perry had come back with the horses, but not the wagon. Otto wondered how long he had been asleep on his feet.

The sky was beginning to lighten as the Poacher led the Count and horses into a bramble patch. Otto remembered this patch. The patch seemed to remember him too. The same thorn raked the same knuckles. Horses chewed, and men watched the river.

The pirates awoke shortly afterward. After the usual "Arr's" and "Avast's," somebody noticed a cart that appeared to have broken down in the middle of the bridge. A buzz arose. Above the hum could be heard a squawking "It's a trick! It's a trick!" but nobody paid attention.

Two boats detached from the island: one was full of pirates; an empty one was tied astern. The pirates rowed to the bridge, dropped anchor at the stone pier in the middle, and scrambled upward. Straining, they lowered the chest off the cart. Grunting, they lowered it by ropes into the empty boat. It rode low in the water when they were done. Struggling against the current, they towed their prize back to the rock. All of the pirates crowded around as their captain stepped into the aft boat. He opened the lid of the chest.

Screams rent the air. Pirates clawed at their bodies and fled, but their tiny island afforded no protection from the terror that pursued them. Some dove or fell into the river. Others leapt into boats and then jumped, still clawing, into the water. Three V-shaped wakes sped toward the rock. Three spade-shaped tails rose into the pinkish sky. The water frothed. Not a pirate survived. A brilliantly colored bird flew back and forth over the carnage screaming, "Toldja so! Toldja so!" until a great green shape snapped it up like a trout going after flies.

The Count looked curiously at his cook. "What was in the chest?"

"Lead, to make it heavy as gold."

"They would not fear lead. What else?"

"Weasels."

Otto and Perry returned exhausted to the castle, but there would be no catching up on sleep. Rollo was wide awake and too excited about the picnic to wait for his host to take charge. Collaring two of his own knights, he pointed toward the kettle of boiling oil on top of the wall. "That pot up there ain't near big enough to feed all of us! You fellers set up a real campfire fer tomorrow out in that there field!"

"No!" Otto disagreed between yawns. "Put it in the gap four furlongs from the castle!" Steep hills hemmed in the road at that location. Marshland lay at their base.

"Then how'll the white knights git to the picnic?" Rollo asked.

"This will give us more time to prepare our surprise."

"But after we light it, what then?"

Otto groaned. "We will sit on opposite sides and sing campfire songs to each other."

"Fair enough. Do y'all's fellers know all the words to 'Sweet Wendolyn Wench'?"

"Probably."

"How about 'Ninety-nine Buckets of Ale on the Wall'? We git stuck around eighty."

Up the road at the gap, Rollo's knights had set to work, dragging in everything that looked like it might burn. One spotted a rough hut by the bog. "Hey, Bub, think that henhouse is bein' used?"

Sir Bubba ambled over. "Hmm. No feathers. Don't stink much. Must be okay." Down came the henhouse. "How 'bout that rail fence?"

"Busted over there. Posts done rotted. Ain't no good fer a fence." It disappeared into the pile.

"Gimme a hand with this stump."

"Sorta soggy, ain't it, Junior?"

"Won't be when the fire dries it out."

In two hours, a pile of debris fifteen feet high and fifty feet wide straddled the gap. Sirs Junior and Bubba stood back and eyed their work.

"Whoo-ee!" expostulated Bubba. "This'll be the biggest barbecue we'll *ever* see."

"You betcha," agreed his companion. "Ding nigh big enough to roast a yellowfin, I reckon."

"A what?"

"A yellowfin. Some sorta critter I heard tell about from out Cathay way. Big as a house. Looks kinda like a giant pig with buck teeth an' a hose fer a nose it picks up things with."

"A giant nose-pickin' pig? Boy, you'll believe anything, won'tcha!"

Sir Junior paid no attention. "Wonder what yellowfin tastes like."

"Fergit yer yellowfin!" bawled Bubba. "If we don't git this thing lit, won't nobody taste nuthin'!"

105

They pulled out flints and iron, but the fire would not start. Two hours later, they were still at it.

Sir Bubba finally shook his head. "We might just as well mosey back to the castle. Cold cuts today, I guess." Defeated, they left.

They were nearly at the drawbridge when Count Rollo yelled at them from the wall. "Ain't you got that thing lit yet?"

"Cain't! Wood must be wet! A dragon couldn't light that stuff!"

"Oh, really?" boomed a voice overhead.

Sirs Bubba and Junior looked up and pelted across the bridge. Four furlongs behind them, the woodpile roared into flame. The terrified knights stopped in the gateway, huffing and puffing, and turned to watch as a silhouette receded through the air toward Yonder Wood.

"Wonder what dragon tastes like."

"Don't reckon I'm gonna try to find out."

Count Otto watched the fire from his window above the wall. In only two hours he had gotten a barrier built. Two hours later, it was toasted. Flames rose a hundred feet into the air. Embers spiraled upward and caught a breeze coming over the hills. Within minutes, fresh wisps of smoke curled upward from Pigtruffle Thicket.

"Dang!" cursed Sir Rollo from the wall. "No truffles this year, I reckon. But wait! What's that?" White shapes raced from the back of the wood, away from the castle. "Hey, Otto!" he yelled toward the window. "It's the White Knights! They musta saved the truffles!"

Otto had forgotten about the little valley that led into the thicket. "SOUND THE ALARM!" he yelled out the window.

The watchman below him was showing a maid the bugle he had won back that morning. He was too busy recounting his victory, dart by dart, to notice the Count. But the maid was not terribly interested in darts, nor in watchmen for that matter, and she noticed. She tried unsuccessfully to interrupt. Finally she grabbed his horn and blew it herself. His eyes opened wide, but his mouth went shut. Then he saw the Count pointing toward the woods.

"HELP! HELLLLP!" The watchman ran back and forth, flapping his hands until the maid hit him with the bugle.

Yelling soldiers surged to the walls. So did Count Otto.

The White Knights had lost the element of surprise but regrouped behind the burning thicket in about five minutes. They drew into formation, four horses wide and about a hundred deep. Lances pointed toward the town. The formation began to move. Dust boiled from the road, obscuring all but the front ranks charging up the approach to the gateway. On the town wall, Otto's knights fitted arrows to strings and drew back their bows. Rollo's men laid bets on the horses.

Shouting men below pulled the town gates shut and dropped bars into place. "Beware the windlass!" yelled the gatekeeper. He knocked a ratchet free with a hammer, and the spoked capstan became a blur as chain screamed up from the drum. The portcullis clanged down outside the gate. Numerous pairs of hands took to a larger windlass that operated the drawbridge. The span groaned upward and came to rest against the gateway.

The gatekeeper ran to the barred postern gate and tugged two ropes. The wooden ledge outside splashed into the moat as its supporting timbers withdrew into the wall. He yanked one more rope. Sand poured into the zigzag passage. Twenty feet of moat separated stone walls and the thrice-blocked gateway

107

from the surrounding land. The town was sealed.

Count Rollo shook his head. *"Now* how're they gonna git them truffles in here fer the picnic?"

Count Otto closed his eyes. It didn't help. Rollo was still there when he reopened them. "They're surprising us, remember? We can't just let them walk in, or they will know we knew they were coming."

"Oh, yeah."

The attacking force was only forty feet from the moat when the drawbridge lifted. The front rank skidded to a halt. Rearward ranks could not see for the dust. The second rank's lances ran into the first rank's horses, which objected. Men and animals plunged into the water. Two men from the second rank also charged into the moat, but the other two ground to a halt. This made more dust. The third rank had the same problem, as did the fourth. A major traffic jam resulted. Screaming men and animals rolled over each other as they tumbled left and right down the embankments.

Rollo's rubberneckers watched loudly and intently. Otto's men relaxed their bows. The White Knights were doing enough damage to themselves that there was no need to waste arrows.

"SURPRISE!" bellowed Rollo. "DIDJ'ALL RESCUE THE TRUFFLES?" An arrow flew up from the melee. He ducked behind the parapet. "Well, just 'cause we ruined their surprise don't mean they have to git all snippy about it." One of his men, Sir Skeeter, apparently felt the same way and threw a rock. It felled the archer with a clang.

"Dinged if I didn't scuff his paint job," drawled Skeeter.

The surviving attackers disentangled themselves and withdrew about three hundred yards. They reformed into a single broad front. Behind them, a row of wagons emerged from the smoke of the thicket and spread out along the length of the front.

"Danged if them ain't the birdwatchers!" breathed Rollo.

Otto turned his head. "Birdwatchers? In covered wagons?"

Rollo nodded, still watching. "Yep. Driver told me folks in the back wanted to watch some kinda night bird. Flagrant flummox, I think he called it. Folks'ud sleep all day in the wagons an' watch birds all night. Wouldn't catch 'em, though. Don't make no sense."

The knights advanced again, but at walking speed. The line stopped just beyond bowshot. Men unloaded rowboats and coils of rope from the wagons.

"Must be a water bird," mused Rollo.

A little way down the wall, a couple of his men watched the same scene. They had not been privy to the discussion between Rollo and the wagon driver.

"What're they doin?" asked Sir Bubba.

Sir Junior studied the scene. "Dunno. Might be one o' them trial thongs."

"A what?"

"Trial thongs. Sortuva Greek race. First they race horses. Then it looks like they're gonna race boats. After that, mebbe they'll race over the walls with them grapplin' hooks. First one over the top wins."

Bubba shook his head slowly. "Where do y'all come *up* with these crazy ideas?"

"Ain't so crazy. I saw it on a vase once my daddy picked up down south."

"If you say so. But I'm sure glad them guys're on our side."

"Yep."

Bubba and Junior silently watched the preparations below

them while Otto's soldiers set piles of stones and buckets of hot oil along the parapet. There was not nearly enough to fend off the attacking force.

"So, Junior, y'all's daddy wuz a knight too?"

"Yep."

What wuz his name?"

"Sir Senior."

"Silly me. Shoulda known. He still knightin'?"

"Nope. Got kilt by a Visigoth."

"Oh. Sorry."

"Don't worry 'bout it. He shoulda known better'n try to say 'Howdy do' in Visigothish. You won't believe what he really said. He said—"

"Don't wanna know."

The second stage of the trial thong was about to begin. The White Knights lashed outriggers to their boats for stability. They set up poles at bow and stern, lashed ridgepoles between them, and stretched water-soaked hides across the boats like pitched roofs. Then they pushed the flotilla into the water, climbed aboard, and set out for the other side of the moat. The defenders fired arrows at them, but the attackers were well shielded. The hidebound boats began to resemble hedgehogs. Otto's forces gave up on archery and dropped torches, stones, and boiling oil instead, but most bounced off the hides and into the water. Very little damage was done except to the defenders, who used up most of their ammunition. The attackers threw off the tarps and prepared to scale the wall.

Otto would have given anything at that moment for a decent moat monster. Then he remembered that he had something better. He leaned over the side of the wall facing the town. Perry was supervising an oil delivery from the kitchen. "Poacher! I need you!"

Perry looked up.

"The handle!" called Otto, pointing toward the gateway.

"Pull the handle!"

Perry nodded and ran into the little room. He tugged at the handle. It would not move. He pulled harder until his feet were off the ground. The lever began to tilt. A sucking noise commenced outside, and the handle suddenly dropped. So did Perry. Bats erupted in a warm black cloud. They returned to their roost as soon as Perry exited.

A ferocious roar erupted from the moat. Horses shied at the noise, and men and animals alike fled. Much of the knightly navy disappeared, boats and all, into the chasm beneath the bridge. A hungry black cloud of displaced mosquitoes began to obscure the swamp. The roar subsided to a gurgle. Shallower water continued to pour across the bottom of the moat, but it did not refill. Knights on shore looked back at the ditch, then up at the wall. Carrying hooks and ropes, they climbed down into the trench.

Two of Rollo's men watched idly, skipping pebbles off attackers. Each stone would make a plinking noise when it bounced off a helmet. Sometimes a stone would ricochet off more than one knight.

"Whoee! Got me a three-plinker, Bubba!"

"Reckon ye did. But I think y'all busted that first helmet."

"Did sound more like a plunk than than a plink, I guess. Shoulda used a littler rock. "Sorry!" Sir Junior called down the wall.

"Hey, Junior."

"Yeah?"

"Wha'd he say?"

"Who?"

"Yore daddy."

"When?"

"To the Visigoth."

Sir Junior drew back, shocked. "Ah cain't tell you that! It's rude!"

111

A short distance down the wall, Otto's Captain of the Guard was less complacent. "Bring oil! Rocks! Anything!" he yelled.

A knight ran into the little room, hoping to find something that had been missed earlier. There were no more stones or oil, though, just bats that did not care about wars and only wanted to go back to sleep. The knight did care about wars but did not care for bats. One flew into his field of vision. He screamed and flailed with his sword. That was counterproductive. The flat of his blade hit the lever by the wall, disturbing bats that had roosted again. They swirled around the knight, and he screamed and flailed more effectively. The lever bounced every time it was hit.

That was productive. The gurgle ceased. The water rose. Knights who had been picking their way across the muddy bottom of the moat fled for the steep sides. Iron boots sink deep in mud, though, and armor does not float.

Men on shore stared. Their sunken comrades flailed like metallic seaweed in a current, but for less than a minute. One dry knight rubbed his mailed arm across his visor to wipe away a tear. It was not effective, so he raised his visor and tried again.

Count Rollo gaped from the castle wall. "He's wearin' a *mask* under his armor!" Indeed he was. "An' they wore white so we'd think they was good guys! CHEATERS!" His bellow echoed from the hills.

The grieving knight lifted his head toward the accusation, beheld Rollo, and in a helpless rage flung his sword at him. It was a very bad throw. The sword sparked against the stone wall and splashed into the water. Rollo's men, who could not tolerate bad sportsmanship, unleashed a volley of fresh arrows and day-old chicken bones.

The attackers retreated out of range. A quarter of their force was dead or wounded, and most of the remainder had lost their zeal. The moat was full, the bridge was up, the portcullis was down, and the postern gate was blocked. The town was safe, at least for the moment.

"Hey, Bub."

"Yeah, Junior?"

"Might as well tell you, I guess. My daddy said—"

A trumpet sounded in the distance. The White Knights turned around. From behind the smoking thicket came a herald preceding a huge white horse, which bore a huge rider in full white armor. The surviving attackers straightened and saluted. Herald, horse, and rider stepped onto the road in front of the smoldering bonfire. The herald stopped there, ceding the road to his lord. The great horse and rider proceeded up the ramp to its end, and stopped. The rider lifted his visor so he would be recognized. He wore no mask.

"Lower the bridge," Otto ordered.

Duke Puckett of Aard stood alone in the middle of the drawbridge, resplendent in his enormous white suit of armor. Powerful by rank, he was also powerful in strength and appetite. The Duke was not composed entirely of lard. Neither was he overly full of humility. Pride, triumph, and greed fought for mastery of his face. His gauntleted right hand gripped a sealed parchment.

Puckett was a villain, but he also was Otto's lord. To

disobey one's lord was tantamount to treason. Count Otto watched from the wall. It was a quiet place. Soldiers around him, having laid down their weapons, studied their lord, his lord on the bridge, and the forces beyond. In the town below them, people had begun to gather as soon as the shooting stopped.

The Count took a deep breath, released it, and descended the stairs into the garrison. A minute later he appeared at the castle door. Townspeople parted just enough for him to walk to the bridge. Friar Fred followed quietly in his wake. The crowd closed behind as spectators strained for a view through the gate. From the watchman's vantage point atop the gatehouse, two heads swam through a sea of heads. The watchman did not notice, of course. If he had, he would have seen two more heads following a short distance behind. One of them belonged to the surly maid. People gave her more clearance than they had given the Count.

Otto stepped onto the bridge. He stopped two paces in front of the Duke. Their eyes locked. Neither man moved.

Impatience crept into the Duke's expression. "Kneel!"

Otto knew he was doomed. Strangely, though, it was a liberating feeling. He looked around for perhaps the last time. White armor ahead of him camouflaged black hearts. Smoke stained the sky above. Contorted iron bodies lined the moat below. Blighted fields to his right stretched toward the swamp. Charred wreckage protruded from the river to his left. Twisting his head to look behind, he saw sparrows flying in and out of castle windows as if they owned the place. Maybe they did. The steep chapel roof marked the spot where Anna and their son lay beneath the floor.

The whispering mob in the muddy street would flee screaming as soon as the row of upright lances pointed their direction, but they could only flee as far as the opposite wall of the town. At the head of the crowd, Perry the Poacher stood beneath the rusty portcullis. The surly maid beside him glanced at the Count with uncharacteristic pity; recovering herself, she bestowed a poisonous glare upon the Duke. Nearer at hand was Friar Fred, as dusty and gray as ever. He and Otto had talked much recently. *Things do get better than this*, thought Otto. He returned his attention to the Duke.

"I kneel only to my betters." The Count pivoted and knelt to the friar. He could hear Puckett sucking air between his teeth.

"You shall die!" roared the livid Duke after Otto arose and faced him again.

"So shall we all, kneeling or no."

"Perhaps you would kneel to your king!" Duke Puckett thrust the parchment forward. "You have no heir to rule after you. I have here a writ sealed by His Majesty, granting me all that is yours!"

Otto was stunned. A minute earlier he had resigned himself to losing everything, but it was a shock nonetheless when it happened. He took the parchment, broke the seal, and stared at it. It certainly had a lot of words. He could not dispute it. He raised his eyes to the Duke. "To the King I would kneel."

"To you I speak as the King. You have ten minutes to set your affairs in order. Then you shall make one last command before I destroy you. Release your Chief Steward from his bondage, and bid him come forward!"

"Ten minutes?"

"Ten minutes, by God, and not a second longer!" The Duke redirected his attention to his line of knights.

"That will be enough." Count Otto had made a decision. "Friar Fred, I shall need you."

The little gray man glanced at the proclamation dangling from Otto's hand, looked again, and began to read in a low voice, "Two tunics, triple extra large, no starch."

Otto stiffened.

"One banner, mend torn corner. Codpiece with wine stain. Tapestry needs new border...."

"Enough foolishness!" Otto muttered. "What drudge could read or write?"

"Friar Florian the Fastidious. He felt called to make the world a cleaner place."

"If you say so. But what of the King's seal?"

"A penny pressed into the wax."

It did not matter. Only the friar could prove the parchment was a fraud. Puckett was judge, and his knights the jury. The verdict was already in, and sentence would be executed in less than ten minutes. Otto called toward the gateway. "Poacher, come here!"

Perry approached. "Yes, my lord?"

"Once I had a son."

Perry dropped his head. "I know, my lord. We were friends."

"You were?"

"Yea, my lord. I was the son of the cook at the crossroad inn. When we were small, I would give my parents the slip on market day and creep into the castle through the herb gate, and we would explore the storerooms. When we were a little older, he would give his governess the slip and eat with us in the kitchen at the inn. When we were older yet, we hunted. He said it was not poaching if he was with me. Later when he took ill, I tried to creep into the castle to see him but was caught and clapped into irons as an intruder."

The Count paused. "Now I wonder if it *was* illness. The Chief Steward had just come. The old one had died. It makes no difference now. Why did you not protest?"

"You did not know me, and you were distracted."

Otto's vision blurred at the memory. Yes, he had been distracted. So had Anna. She had sat in the sunlight of their window and wept until she, too, had died. But enough of that.

He would not spend his last ten minutes mourning. He cleared his throat. "The inn is gone. What of your parents?"

"The plague took them, my lord."

"Well, then." The Count raised his voice. "Friar Fred, I am adopting the orphan Perry the Poacher as my son and heir. As God's witness, I request your blessing."

Perry turned pale. The crowd buzzed. The Duke jolted. The friar blinked and recovered. "Amen. So be it done in the name of the Father, the Son, and the Holy Ghost."

Duke Puckett rounded on the little group. "I forbid it!" he thundered.

"You cannot," countered the friar. "It is done. I answer only to my God and my abbot, in that order."

The deed was done, but Otto was not. "That would seem to make the proclamation invalid."

"It does not!" roared the Duke.

"Let me read it aloud," interjected the friar. "We will see." He raised his voice. "Two tu—"

The Duke snatched the parchment.

Friar Fred faced him. "As you wish. But you swore by God that the Count would have ten minutes to set his affairs in order. Five remain."

The Duke glared.

Otto laid a hand on Perry's shoulder. "Tell me, my son, does yon surly maid have parents?"

"No, my—NO!" Perry regained his color, and then some. "I mean, no, sir, she does not, but you cannot—I mean—"

The barest of smiles creased the Count's face. "You would not have her as a sister?"

"I—we have other plans, my lo—er, Father."

"As I thought. Well, my son cannot marry a commoner. Call her."

Perry called toward the gate. "Yo, Shirley!"

She arrived and planted herself before the Count.

117

"Shirley?" the count asked.

"*Most* surely."

"Then surely shall it be. My cousin Izzi died without issue, and I manage his lands. They are not mine. I now adopt you as his daughter by proxy. All that was his is yours. The Duke will have to ask the King for another proclamation for Izzi's holdings. And Friar Fred, I shall need another blessing."

Shirley's jaw dropped. The Duke opened his mouth.

"Amen-so-be-it-done-in-the-name-of-the-Father-the-Son-and-the-Holy-Ghost," hurried the friar. "Too late, Duke."

The crowd murmured. The Duke spluttered. Otto spoke louder. "Now, my son, you may wed Lady Surly—er, Shirley—in as much peace as she will grant you. But first you have an errand. Bring me the Chief Steward."

The two newest members of the nobility hurried toward the castle. Perry gestured toward the gateway as they passed through it, and Shirley shook her head.

He pointed at the excited crowd. "No, they will need you. And it will not be for long anyway."

"Pip-pip, Lord Pirrip!" somebody in the crowd shouted. There were cheers.

"Surly girlie, Lady Shirley!" somebody else chanted.

Shirley stopped cold. The crowd became deathly silent. Perry continued to the castle.

The Duke roared at Count Otto, "You fool! Your game changes nothing! They will die!"

"Would they have lived otherwise?" countered the Count.

"Of course not!"

"So we have lost nothing. But why do you so desire this county, my lord? It is far from your estates, and we have little."

The Duke smirked. "It will not be far after I expand my estates for *my* heirs. And a Count should not have a fine dragon when his Duke has only an Aardvark." He gazed toward Yonder Wood.

118

As if one could have *a dragon!* thought Otto. But he would play along. "Ah, now it makes sense. To steal my county and my dragon—"

The Duke continued to watch the wood. "Not steal. I am your lord."

"I am corrected, my lord. To deceitfully snatch—not steal, my lord, but snatch—what you were entitled to, your men secretly prepared in Count Rollo's county and sought to attack me by surprise. I suppose you are entitled to murder Rollo as well, my lord. But he is harmless. Why have you sought to kill him?"

"He knows too much."

"Too much what?" The subject of the discussion had strolled onto the bridge with a half-eaten chicken leg in his hand.

"Never mind," muttered Otto through the side of his mouth. "Rollo, go tell the cook you want dessert."

"Reckon I do. Say howdy to His Duckiness fer me." Rollo ambled back into town, finishing his chicken.

Perry had not yet come back. Otto was glad of that. Every minute of stalling was another minute that his subjects would live, and another minute to bait the Duke. "And why do you want my Steward? Have you not enough villains of your own?"

The Duke whirled. "Fool! Dare not call him villain! He ruled your castle at my bidding these last two years."

"So I shall call him a spy instead."

"That's better."

"And a murderer," Count Otto said.

The Duke glowered.

"Did you plot his imprisonment also?" the Count asked.

"No, he brought that upon himself for insulting me. But he remained loyal and served me even from his cell."

"Indeed." Otto frowned. "And if I had demanded his head?"

"He would have told your headsman where to find my

119

ring. Your 'Steward' is—"

But there was no more discussion of the subject. Perry had returned, leading the Chief Steward by the hand. The pale man blinked in the sunlight and shuffled toward the bridge. He wiped his eyes with his free hand, peered ahead, and spotted the Duke. "Papa?"

The Duke gasped. The Chief Steward tore free from Perry and loped forward with his arms outstretched, gibbering with joy. No sooner had he come within reach than the Duke flung him aside.

The Steward teetered at the edge of the bridge, eyes wide in amazement. "Papa?"

"I have no son."

The Chief Steward's mouth hung open in disbelief. He said nothing more but crumpled backward. A splash was followed by a tumult below the bridge. Red stains erupted in the water. A young monster, freshly sucked in from the river, was on patrol.

The Friar prayed as quickly as he could, hoping to complete the Last Rites before the creature swallowed. The Duke stood riveted to his spot, as pale as his armor and as still as a stone. Perry the Poacher flung himself sobbing onto the bridge deck, with his arms reaching over the side toward the man he could not save. The monster snapped at him but was out of range. Its head arched downward and disappeared into the bloody water, followed by twenty feet of neck and sinuous body. A green tail flipped through the air and receded as the serpent resumed its rounds.

Finally the Duke moved. "But I shall have a dragon!" He maneuvered past the Count so he could see both him and the white line of knights. He would have just enough time to exact personal vengeance and get out of the way before the first lancers thundered onto the bridge. "Have you any last words?" he sneered.

"Yes, but not to you." Count Otto bowed his head. His lips moved in prayer. *I'm ready, Papa. May I come home now?*

Enraged, Duke Puckett lifted his sword high with both hands. Lances lowered. Horsemen charged forward, hot for vengeance.

Back in the town, a woman shouted commands. Soldiers on the wall scrambled for their weapons. The gates began to close. Lady Shirley pelted toward the narrowing opening with a sword ahead of her, but she was too late. Only the blade penetrated the gap. She could be heard screaming and pounding on the gates from the inside. The portcullis crashed down between the gate and the bridge.

The Duke gathered his strength and prepared to split the Count from top to bottom.

Then a shadow blocked the sun, and Count Otto heard a voice inside his head say, *"Not yet, son."*

"Ooh! A marshmallow!" called a voice from the sky.

A blast of flame followed, and the rotund Duke's brilliant white armor was instantly transformed into a smoking black crust. His red-hot sword slipped from charred gauntlets and clanged off the bridge. It sank with a squealing hiss and a puff of steam. The swooping dragon slurped up the Duke and settled to earth on the far bank amidst a clatter of scaly wings. It chewed a couple of times, then spat the helmet into the moat. All other potential marshmallows fled except for those flattened by the landing.

The dragon sighed with toothy contentment. "Just the way I like them! Crunchy on the outside, tender on the inside."

Don't Miss…

Heavens to Louie
DON BEMIS

Whoever said that living in a small town was boring?…

Louie is really good at dreaming up bad ideas.

You know the type: the person you think really needs God's help, but you don't know what to do with him when he shows up at church.

When Louie accidentally sabotages a Christmas pageant, he decides he needs to shape up. But every effort only creates more chaos. Is it possible for a guy like Louie to change?

Stop by Floyd's Fountain for bad coffee and worse food. Stay long enough to meet Louie, Bob, Miss Phelps, Percy the Motorcycle Bum, and the others. And discover why there's a place even for the Louies of the world.

Charmingly homespun, hysterical, and poignant… with just a touch of romance too.

About the Author

DON BEMIS set out to be a city planner but has worked in engineering nearly all of his adult life. He was born in Carlsbad, New Mexico, and graduated with a BS in geography from New Mexico State University.

Count Otto's Dragon is Don's second book. It bears no connection to his first one, *Heavens to Louie* (a charmingly homespun story you won't want to miss), except that they share an author with a somewhat warped sense of humor. The book originated as an opening sentence for submittal to the Bulwer-Lytton competition for wretched literature.

"It was never submitted," Don says, "but my wife, Lois, told me, 'Now you have to turn it into a book.'" So Don decided to see just how flowery he could paint a dismal scene, and the sentence grew by several paragraphs.

The rest is history. Not true history, though.

Don and Lois live in a century-old house in South Haven, Michigan, where Don is employed full-time at a nuclear power plant after wandering around the country for three years as an engineering consultant. He was just elected as a write-in candidate to the City Council, which is not difficult if nobody else wants the job enough to run. When Don isn't writing or pottering around a power plant, he may be playing his clarinet, woodworking, or teaching adult Sunday school. He and Lois have five adult children and two grandchildren.

For more information:
www.donbemis.com www.oaktara.com